Esaias Tegnér, Thomas A.E Holcomb, Martha A Lyon Holcomb

Fridthjof's Saga

A Norse Romance. Third Edition

Esaias Tegnér, Thomas A.E Holcomb, Martha A Lyon Holcomb

Fridthjof's Saga
A Norse Romance. Third Edition

ISBN/EAN: 9783744766746

Printed in Europe, USA, Canada, Australia, Japan

Cover: Foto ©Andreas Hilbeck / pixelio.de

More available books at **www.hansebooks.com**

FRIDTHJOF'S SAGA;

A NORSE ROMANCE,

BY

ESAIAS TEGNÉR,

BISHOP OF WEXIÖ.

TRANSLATED FROM THE SWEDISH

BY

THOMAS A. E. HOLCOMB AND MARTHA A. LYON HOLCOMB.

THIRD EDITION.

CHICAGO:
S. C. GRIGGS AND COMPANY.
LONDON: TRÜBNER & CO.
1892.

KNIGHT & LEONARD, PRINTERS, CHICAGO.

Electrotyped by
A. ZEESE & CO., CHICAGO.

a

NOTE BY THE TRANSLATORS.

TEGNÉR'S poem, "Fridthjof's Saga," has been printed in Sweden in many large editions and in almost every possible style. It has been illustrated, and it has been set to music. It has been translated into nearly all the modern European languages. Moreover it has been rendered into English by eighteen different translators, and has been twice reprinted in America. Bayard Taylor edited an American edition of a translation by Rev. William L. Blackley of Dublin, and published it about ten years ago. Professor R. B. Anderson has just published in his "Viking Tales," a translation made by Professor George Stephens of Copenhagen, and which received the sanction of Bishop Tegnér himself.

And yet we venture to add another, and present here the *first complete American* translation. Mr. Taylor said in his preface to Blackley's version that there had never been an English Fridthjof's Saga which was satisfactory to Swedes. This is probably owing to the fact that the Swedes have become so familiar with its original measures and so accustomed to its peculiar rhythm, that they cannot willingly dispense with any part of the form which Tegnér gave it. Several of the metres employed by him were unknown to Swedish readers until they appeared in this poem. Tegnér's experiment of introducing them was a successful one; and they are now, in the minds of Swedes, as much a part of the work as the story itself. The feminine rhymes, occurring in fifteen of the twenty-four cantos, are so melodious that no one who had heard the original, even if he did not understand a word of it, could be quite satisfied with a version which does not reproduce them. The feminine rhymes, and the alliteration of Canto XXI, have presented obstacles which no single translation has hitherto overcome.

The original measures, the feminine rhymes and the alliteration of " Ring's Drapa," are, in our estimation, essential features of a good rendering of the poem, and if we have done our work well we do not fear that any one will think there are too many translations.

For a fuller history of " Fridthjof's Saga " than can be given in this note, we refer the reader to Anderson's " Viking Tales," where the sagas on which this story is founded appear in full.

The preparation of this translation has been a home work which has brightened for us the firelight of many a pleasant evening. We publish it in full faith that it will have a like happy effect in whatever home it may be read.

October, 1876.

CONTENTS.

CHARACTERS.

Bele. *(Pronounced Bä'-lä.)* King of Sogn, in Norway.

Helge *(Hel'-gä)* and **Halfdan.** His sons.

Ingeborg. *(Ing'-e-borg.)* His daughter.

Thorstein. *(Tor'-stine.)* A peasant, — friend and companion-in-arms of king BELE.

Fridthjof. *(Freet'-yof.)* Son of THORSTEIN.

Hilding. Foster-father and teacher of FRIDTHJOF and INGEBORG.

Bjorn. *(B'yorn.)* A sworn foster-brother of FRIDTHJOF.

Ring. King of Ringric, in Norway.

Angantyr. *(Ang'-an-teer.)* Ruler of the Orkney Islands.

Atle. *(At'-lä.)* A berserk, and one of ANGANTYR's warriors.

SCENE — Northern Norway and the Orkney Islands.

FRIDTHJOF'S SAGA.

I.

FRIDTHJOF AND INGEBORG.

IN Hilding's garden, green and fair,
  Protected by his fostering care,
Two rare and stately plants were growing,
Unequaled grace and beauty showing.

The one a sturdy oak tree grew,
With lance-like stem so straight and true,
Its crown in northern tempests shaking
Like helmet plume in battle quaking.

The other like a rose sprang forth
When tardy winter leaves the north,
And spring, which in the buds lies dreaming,
Still waits with gems to set them gleaming.

Around the earth the storm-king raves,

The wrestling oak its anger braves;

The sun dissolves frost's mantle hoary,

The buds reveal their hidden glory.

So they grew up in joy and glee,

And Fridthjof was the young oak tree;

Unfolding in the vale serenely,

The rose was Ingeborg the queenly.

Saw you those two by light of day

You seem in Freyja's house to stay,

Where bride-pairs, golden-haired, were swinging,

Their way on rosy pinions winging.

But seeing them by moonlight pale

Round-dancing in the leafy vale,

You'd think: The elf-king now advances,

And leads his queen in fairy dances.

How joyful 'twas, how lovely too,

When first he learned his futhorc through;

No kings had e'er such honor brought them .

As when to Ingeborg he taught them.

How joyously his boat would glide
With those two o'er the dark blue tïde;
While he the driving sail was veering,
Her small white hands gave hearty cheering.

No bird's nest found so high a spot,
That he for her could find it not;
The eagle's nest from clouds he sundered,
And eggs and young he deftly plundered.

However swift, there ran no brook,
But o'er it Ingeborg he took;
How sweet when roaring torrents frighten,
To feel her soft arms round him tighten.

The first spring flowers by sunshine fed,
The earliest berries turning red,
The first of autumn's golden treasure,
He proffered her with eager pleasure.

*   *   *   *   *   *

But quickly sped are childhood's days,—
There stands a youth whose ardent gaze
With pleading and with hope is laden,
And there, with budding charms, a maiden.

Young Fridthjof followed oft the chase,
Which led to many a fearful place;
With neither spear nor lance defended,
The wild bear's life he quickly ended.

When, struggling, met they breast to breast,
The hunter won, though hardly pressed,
And brought the bearskin home; such prizes,
Think you, a maiden e'er despises?

For woman values courage rare;
(The brave alone deserves the fair, \
Each one the other's grace completing,
As brow and helmet fitly meeting.

And when in winter evenings long,
By firelight reading, in a song,
Of fair abodes in radiant heaven
To every god and goddess given,

He thought: "Of gold is Ing'borg's hair,
A net for rose and lily fair;
Like Freyja's bounteous golden tresses,
A wheat-field which the breeze caresses.

Fair Idun's beauteous bosom beats
Beneath the green silk's safe retreats,—
I know a silk whose sheen encloses
Light · fairies two, with buds of roses.

And Frigg's mild eyes are blue and clear
As heaven, when no clouds appear,—
But I know eyes beside whose sparkles
A light, blue spring day quickly darkles.

And Gerd's fair cheeks, why praise them so?
The northern-lights on new fall'n snow,—
I know of cheeks whose rosy warnings
Portray at once two ruddy mornings.

I know a heart affection-crowned
Like Nanna's, though not so renowned;
And Nanna's love, in song and story,
Is justly reckoned Balder's glory.

For oh, what joy when death appears,
To have a faithful maiden's tears!
To prove a love so strong and tender,
With Hel's grim shades I'd gladly wander."

Meanwhile the princess gayly wove
In cloth, blue wave and greenest grove;
And as she sang a hero's story,
She also wove a hero's glory.

For soon there grew in snow-white wool
Bright shields from off the golden spool,
Here, red prevail the battle lances,
There, silver-stiffened armor glances.

Anon her fingers deftly trace
A hero,—see, 'tis Fridthjof's face;
And though at first almost affrighted,
She blushes, smiles and is delighted.

The birch tree's stem where Fridthjof went
Showed I and F in beauty blent;
As grew those runes in one, delighted,
So too those hearts in one united.

When Day invests the upper air,
The world-king with the golden hair,
When men to action urge each other,
They think alone of one another.

When Night pervades the upper air,
The world-queen with the raven hair,
When stars in silence greet each other,
They dream alone of one another.

"Thou Earth, who in the spring-time fair,
Bedeck'st with flowers thine emerald hair,
Give me the best; in wreaths I'll wind them,
And round my Fridthjof's brow will bind them."

"Thou sea, who mak'st thy dark caves bright
With myriad pearls' refulgent light,
Give me the best; I'll weave the clearest
A necklace for my Ing'borg dearest."

"Thou ornament of Odin's throne,
Eye of the world, O golden sun,
Wert thou but mine, thy blazing splendor
I'd give a shield to my defender."

"Thou guide in Odin's house at night,
Thou pale moon with thy lovely light,
Wert thou but mine, thy pearly lustre
'Mid Ing'borg's golden hair should cluster."

But Hilding said: "My foster-son,
Your reason is by love outrun;
The norns are partial in bestowing
The blood that in her veins is flowing.

To Odin high, where bright stars shine,
Ascendeth her ancestral line;
No hope may son of Thorstein nourish,
For like with like alone can flourish."

But Fridthjof smiled: "My race," he said,
"Goes down unto the valiant dead;
The forest-king I slew, and merit
Thereby, the honor kings inherit.

"The free-born man will never yield,
He owns the world's unconquered field;
For fate can bind what she has broken,
And hope is crowned with kingly token.

"All power is noble; Thor presides
In Thrudvang, where all strength abides;
There worth, and not descent, is leader,—
The sword is e'er a valiant pleader.

"I'd fight the world for my sweet bride,
Yea, though the thunder-god defied.
Be glad and brave, my lily, never
Shall mortal dare our lives to sever."

II.

KING BELE AND THORSTEIN.

KING Bele, sword-supported, in the palace stood;
And with him Thorstein, Viking's son, the peasant good,
His ancient war companion, grown old in glory,
His brow was scarred like rune-stones, his hair was hoary.

They stood, as on the mountain two temples stand
To honored gods devoted, now half in sand;
And many words of wisdom the walls are saying,
And holy recollections through domes are straying.

"The evening steals upon me," king Bele said,
"The helmet now is heavy, and stale the mead;
The fate of man grows darker, but all the clearer
High Valhal shines before me, as death draws nearer.

"My sons I here have summoned, and Thorstein's son;
For they should cling together, as we have done;
But I would give the eaglets some words of warning —
Words may in death be sleeping ere dawns the morning."

Obedient to the mandate, the three advance —
First, Helge, dark and gloomy, with sullen glance;
He dwelt amid diviners; the hand he proffered
Was red with blood of victims, on altars offered.

The next who came was Halfdan, a light-haired swain;
His countenance was noble, but weak and vain;
He gaily bore a falchion, with which he gestured,
And seemed a youthful maiden, in armor vestured.

And after them came Fridthjof, in mantle blue;
He was stronger than the others, and taller, too;
He stood between the brothers, by contrast seeming
Like noon 'twixt night and morning, in splendor beaming.

"Ye sons," the king said gently, "my sun goes down;
Together rule the kingdom and take the crown;
For unity is power, and no endeavor,
While lance with ring is circled, its stem can sever.

"Let power stand as sentry on every hand,
And freedom bloom protected throughout the land;
The sword is for protection, and not for plunder,
And shields are locks for peasants no foe can sunder.

"How foolish is the ruler his land to oppress,

For the people give the power which kings possess;

The crown of leafy verdure which decks the mountain

Will wither if the sunshine dries up the fountain.

"On four gigantic pillars is heaven's throne —

The throne of nations resteth on law alone;

Destruction waits on judgment if misdirected;

By right are men ennobled and kings perfected.

"In Disarsal, O Helge, the high gods dwell —

Not pinioned as the snail is within his shell;

As far as daylight flieth, or thought's swift pinion,

Far as resound the echoes, is gods' dominion.

"The offered hawk gives tokens which oft deceive.

Not all runes monumental can we believe;

But an honest heart, O Helge, of pure endeavor,

With Odin's runes is written, misleading never.

"Be not severe, king Helge, but firm and staid;

The sword that bites the sharpest has the limberest blade.

Kings are adorned by mercy, as shields by flowers,

And spring can more accomplish than winter's powers.

"A man, however mighty, deprived of friends,

Like tree of bark denuded, how soon life ends!

But he by friends surrounded, like trees shall flourish,

Whose crowns, in groves protected, the brooklets nourish.

"Boast not ancestral wisdom; each man alone

A single bowstring uses, and that his own;

What matters it to any the worth that's buried?

By its own waves the current o'er seas is carried.

"A joyous spirit, Halfdan, advantage brings,

But idle talk is needless, and most, to kings;

Of hops, as well as honey, is mead compounded,

Let sports on vigor, lances on steel, be founded.

"No man has too much wisdom, though learned he be,

And much too little, many less learned than he;

To fools, though high in station, no praise is meted,

The wise by all are honored, though lowly seated.

"The steadfast friend, O Halfdan! of mingled blood,

Lives near indeed, though distant be his abode;

But to thy foeman's dwelling the way is weary,—

Though standing by thy pathway, 'tis far and dreary.

"For friend choose not the first one that's so disposed,—
An empty house stands open, a full one closed;
Choose one, the best, O Halfdan, nor seek another,
The world soon knows the secrets of three together."

These words then Thorstein uttered in clearest tone:
"King Bele unto Odin goes not alone;
We've always stood together, whatever tried us,
And death, now drawing near, shall not divide us.

"Fridthjof, old age hath whispered in my rapt ear
Full many words of wisdom, which thou must hear.
Birds fly from graves to Odin, with wisdom freighted,
The words by old men spoken, should not be slighted.

"First, give the high gods honor; for good or ill,
Storms come as well as sunshine, by Heaven's will.
The gods perceive the secrets in thy possession,
And years must make atonement for each transgression.

"Obey the king: most wisely rules one alone,
The eyes of night are many, day has but one.
The better are contented by best directed,—
The blade must have a handle to be perfected.

"Great strength is heaven's dower; but, Fridthjof, learn
That power devoid of wisdom, can little earn.
Strong bears by one are taken,—one man of reason;
Set shields to turn the sword stroke, let law stop treason.

"A few may fear the haughty, whom all despise,
And with the proud in spirit, destruction lies:
Those once flew high, who're now on crutches creeping;
The winds rule fortune, weather, time of reaping.

"The day thou'lt rightly prize, whose sun has sunk,
Advice when it is followed, and ale when drunk.
The hopes of youth on shadows are often rested,
But strength of sword and friendship, by use are tested.

"Trust not the snow of spring-time, nor night-old ice;
The serpent when he sleepeth, nor girl's advice;
The mind of changeful woman not long abideth,
And fickleness of spirit, 'neath flower-tints hideth.

"All men will surely perish with all they prize,
But one thing know I, Fridthjof, which never dies,—
And that is reputation! therefore, ever
The noble action strive for, the good endeavor."

So warned the aged chieftains in the palace hall.

As since the skald has chanted in Hávamál,

So passed these sayings pithy through generations;

And still from graves they whisper 'mid northern nations.

Then many words and heartfelt, these warriors found

To tell their lasting friendship, so wide renowned.

How friends till death, if fortune or frowned or slighted,

Like two hands clasped together they stood united.

"And back to back in battle we held the field,

And which way norns did threaten, they smote a shield;

Before you now to Valhal we old men hasten,

And may their fathers' spirit our children's chasten."

The king said much concerning brave Fridthjof's worth,

Heroic power surpassing all royal birth;

And much was said by Thorstein, how graces cluster

Round Northland's honored monarchs, with Asa-lustre.

"But hold ye fast together, ye children three,

The Northland then your conqueror shall never see;

For royalty and power, when duly ordered,

Are like a bright shield golden, by blue steel bordered.

"Salute my daughter Ing'borg, the rosebud sweet,
In quiet was she nurtured, as seemed meet;
Protect her, lest the storm-king, with cruel power,
Should fasten in his helmet my tender flower.

"I lay on thee, king Helge, a father's care,
Love Ing'borg as a daughter, the jewel rare!
Restraint galls noble spirits, but gentle manner
Will lead both man and woman to right and honor.

"But lay us now, ye children, in two mound-graves,
Close where the blue gulf tosses its ceaseless waves;
Our souls shall then forever enjoy the ringing
Of dirges which in breaking the waves are singing.

"When the moon's pale beams the mountains and valleys fill,
And midnight's dew is falling on grove and hill;
Then will we sit, O Thorstein, above our pillows,
And talk about the future, across the billows.

"And now, farewell, ye children, our work is done;
Unto the Allfather gladly we hasten on,
Like weary rivers longing for sea's caressing;
On you be Thor's and Odin's and Frey's rich blessing."

2

III.

FRIDTHJOF'S INHERITANCE.

BURIED were Bele and Thorstein together, as they had commanded;

High rose their grave-mounds on each side the gulf by the blue rolling water,

Death having sundered the hearts that in life were so closely united.

Helge and Halfdan, by will of the people, took jointly the kingdom

Left by their father; but Fridthjof, an only son, heired alone Framness,

Took unmolested possession, and settled himself there in quiet.

Stretching around him for twelve miles unbroken his acres extended;

Three sides were dale, hill and mountain, the fourth side looked out on the ocean;

Crowned were the hill-tops with forests of birch-wood, but, on their sides sloping,

Golden corn plentiful grew, and like billows the tall rye
was waving.

Many in number the lakes which their mirrors held up
for the mountains;

Held them up, too, for the woods in whose thickets the
high-horned elks wandered,

Making there kingly roads, drinking from running brooks
counted by hundreds.

But in the valleys wide, on the smooth greensward were
quietly grazing

Glossy-skinned herds, which with udders distended now
long for the milk-pail.

Scattered among them were myriads of white-wooled
sheep, constantly moving,

Looking like fleecy clouds sailing serenely across the
blue heavens,

Wafted now hither now thither in crowds by the winds
in the spring-time.

Twelve times two coursers, fierce whirlwinds, defiant
though fettered,

Stood in the rows of stalls, stamping and restless, the
meadow-hay chewing,

Knotted their long manes with red, and their hoofs
    were with iron shoes glistening.
Standing apart was the drinking-hall, built of the choic-
    est fir timber;
Counting ten twelves to the hundred, not five hundred
    warriors assembled
Filled up the spacious apartment, when all met to drink
    mead at Yule-time.
Down through the middle, from end to end, ran a
    strong table of stone-oak,
Polished with wax and like steel shining; carved on
    two pillars of elm-wood,
Far at one end, Frey and Odin supported the dais of honor,
Odin with lordly look, Frey with the sun for a crest on
    his bonnet.
'Twixt the two, on a bear-skin (black as a coal was
    this bear-skin,
Scarlet the mouth, while the tips of the claws were with
    bright silver shining),
Thorstein among his friends sat — Hospitality minister-
    ing to Gladness.
Oft when the moon in the heavens was riding, the old
    man related

Wonders of foreign lands seen by him when as a viking
    he journeyed,

Far on the waves of the Baltic, the White, and the
    Northern seas tossing.

Mutely the company listened. Fixed were their eyes on
    the speaker,

Even as bees upon roses; the poet was thinking of Brage,*

Brage with silver beard flowing, and tongue clothed in
    wisdom the choicest,

Sitting 'neath shadowy birches, telling a story by Mimer's

Unceasingly murmuring fountain, he too a saga unending.

Covered with straw was the floor, and upon a walled
    hearth in the center,

Constantly burned, warm and cheerful, a fire, while
    down the wide chimney

Twinkling stars, heavenly friends, glanced upon guest
    and hall, quite unforbidden.

Studded with nails were the walls, and upon them were
    hanging

Helmets and coats-of-mail closely together; also between
    them

* Bra-ge (two syllables).

Here and there flashed down a sword, like a meteor
　　shooting at evening.

Brighter than helmet or sword were the sparkling shields
　　ranged round the chamber;

Bright as the face of the sun were they, clear as the
　　moon's disc of silver.

Oft as the horns needed filling, there passed round the
　　table a maiden;

Modestly blushing she cast down her eyes, her beautiful
　　image

Mirrored appeared in the shields, and gladdened the
　　heart of each warrior.

Rich was the house, and the eye of the stranger, which-
　　ever way gazing,

Rested on cellar well filled, or on pantry or press over-
　　flowing.

Jewels the rarest, trophies of conquest, gleamed in pro-
　　fusion;

Gold carved in runes with great skill, and wonderful
　　things wrought in silver.

Chief in this limitless treasure three things were most
　　of all valued.

First of the three was a sword, which from sire and
from grandsire descended,
Called *Angervadil*, or grief-wader, sometimes, too, brother
of lightning.
Far, far away in the East it was forged — so at least
says the story —
Tempered in fire by the dwarfs, Bjorn Bluetooth the
first one who bore it.
Bjorn lost at once both the sword and his life in a
bravely-fought battle,
Southward in Groning Sound, where he struggled with
Vifil the powerful.
Vifil's possessions descended to Viking.
                                        At Woolen-Acre,
Old and infirm, there lived a great king with a beautiful
daughter.
See, from the depths of the forest there cometh a giant
misshapen,
Higher in stature than man, a monster ferocious and
shaggy,
Boldly demanding a hand-to-hand combat, or kingdom
and daughter.

No one, however, accepted the challenge, for none had a
    weapon
Able his hard skull to pierce, and therefore they called
    him the Iron-skull.
Viking, whose winters scarce fifteen had numbered, nobly
    advancing,
Entered the fray, secure in his strong arm and good
    Angervadil,   ·
Cleft at one blow the hideous goblin, and rescued the
    maiden.
Viking bequeathed the good weapon to Thorstein, his
    son, and Thorstein,
To Odin ascended, bequeathed it to Fridthjof. Whenever
    he drew it,
Light filled the hall as when northern lights entered, or
    lightning flashed through it.
Hammered of gold was the hilt, with strange letters 'twas
    covered;
Wonderful mysteries were they in Northland, but known
    to the people
Who dwell near the gates of the sun, where our fathers
    lived ere they came hither.

Faint were the runes when the land was in quiet
　　throughout all its borders;
But when the followers of Hild were summoned, then
　　were they burning
Red as the comb of a cock when he fighteth.　Lost
　　was the warrior
Who met, on the field of encounter, the blade with its
　　red letters glowing.
Widely renowned was that sword, and of swords was the
　　chief in the Northland.　　　　　　　　——— .

Next highly prized was a ponderous *arm-ring*, widely
　　notorious,
Forged by the Vulcan of northern tradition, the halting
　　smith Volund;
Three marks it weighed, and gold was the metal of
　　which it was fashioned;
Carved were the heavens with twelve towering castles,
　　where dwell the immortals,—
Emblem of changing months, called by the poets the
　　sun's glorious dwelling.
First there was Frey's castle Alfheim, that is the sun,
　　which born newly,

Starts once again to ascend the steep pathway of Heaven
    at Yule-time.

There too was Sokvabek; seated within it were Odin and
    Saga

Drinking together their wine from a gold shell,— that
    shell is the Ocean,

Colored with gold from the glow of the morning. Saga
    is Spring-time,

Writ on the green of the fresh springing field, with
    flowers for letters.

Balder, the kingly, is pictured there, throned on the sun
    at midsummer,

Which pours from the firmament riches untold,— per-
    sonified goodness;

For lights are the good, radiant, resplendent, but the
    evil are darkness.

Constantly rising the sun groweth weary; the good also
    falter,

Giddy with walking precipitous heights; sighing they
    downward

Sink to the land of the shades,— down to Hel. That is
    of Balder

The funeral pile. Glitner, the castle of Peace, is there; seated

Within it was Forsété,* scales in hand, meting out justice.

Many more pictures with these there engraven, betoken the conflict

Waged against darkness, on earth and in heaven; bright were they shining,

Wrought by a master's hand on the broad arm-ring. Clustering rubies

Crown its high center, e'en as in summer the sun crowns the heavens.

Long was the circlet a family heir-loom. On the side of the mother

Traced they their pedigree back to old Volund, ancestor mighty.

Once, says tradition, the jewel was stolen by robber named Soti,

Roaming abroad through the seas. Long was it ere 'twas recovered.

Finally (so runs the story) 'twas said that the robber had buried

Himself with his ship, and his treasure, deep on the far coast of Britain.

* For-se-te.

Pleasure or quiet he found not, a ghost was his irksome
  companion.

Hearing the rumor, Thorstein with Bele the dragon ship
  mounted,

Dashed through the foaming waves, straight to the place
  of the sepulcher steering.

Wide as a temple's arch, or a king's gateway, bedded in
  gravel,

Covered with grassy turf, arched to the top, the tomb
  rose forbidding.

Light issued from it. Through a small crevice within
  the closed portal,

Peered the two champions. There the pitched viking ship

Stood with its masts, its yards and its anchor. High in
    the stern sheets

Was seated a terrible figure, clad in a mantle all flaming,

Furious demon scouring a blade that with blood spots
  was covered.

Vain was his labor, naught could remove them. All his
    rich booty

Round him was scattered, and on his arm was the ring
  he had stolen.

"Go we," said Bele, "down thither and fight with the
hideous goblin,

Two 'gainst a spirit of fire." But Thorstein half angrily
answered:

"One against one is the rule of our fathers. I fight well
singly."

Long they contended which first of the two the encounter
should venture,

Proving the perilous journey. Bele at last took his
helmet,

Shaking two lots therein. Watched by the stars Thorstein
saw by their shimmer

His was the lot first appearing. A blow from his javelin
of iron

Cleft the huge bolts and strong locks. He descended.
Did any one question

What was revealed in the cavern, then was he silent and
shuddered.

Bele at first heard strange music. It rang like the song
of a goblin;

Then was a clattering noise, like the clashing of blades
in a combat,

Lastly a hideous shriek,—then silence. Out staggered
    Thorstein,

Confounded, bewildered, all pale was his face, for with
    death had he battled;

Yet bore he the arm-ring a trophy. " 'Twas dear bought,"
    he often said frowning;

" Once in my life was I frightened; 'twas when I recovered
    that arm-ring."

Widely renowned was that ring, and of rings was the
    chief in the Northland.

Lastly the ship, called *Ellide*, was one of the family jewels.

Viking, so say they, returning triumphant from venture-
    some journeys,

Sailed along coasting near Framness. There he espied on
    a shipwreck,

Carelessly swinging, a sailor, sporting as 'twere with the
    billows.

Noble of figure, tall in his stature, joyful his visage,

Changeable too, like the waves of the sea when they sport
    in the sunshine,—

Blue was his mantle, golden his girdle and studded with
    corals;

Sea-green his hair, but his beard was as white as the foam
of the ocean.

Viking his serpent steered thither to rescue the unfortunate
stranger,—

Took him half frozen to Framness, and there as a guest
entertained him.

When by his host to repose he was bidden, smiling he
answered:

"Fair sits the wind, and my ship which you boarded, is
not yet disabled;

Long ere the morning I trust she will bear me a hundred miles seaward.

Thanks for thy bidding, 'twas well meant and kindly.
Ah! could I only

Leave thee a gift to remind thee of me! but afar on the
ocean

Lieth my kingdom. Perhaps in the morning 'twill waft
thee a token."

Viking next day by the sea-shore was standing, when
lo! like an eagle

Madly pursuing its prey, a dragon ship sailed into har-
bor.

Nowhere was visible sailor or captain, or even a steers-
man;

Winding 'mid rocks and through breakers, the rudder a
path sought unaided;

When the firm strand it was nearing, sudden, as ruled
by a spirit,

Reefed were the sails unassisted. Untouched by finger
of mortal,

The anchor sped through the clear water and fastened
its barbs in the bottom.

Viking gazed, speechless with wonder; the sportive
winds sang in low cadence:

"Æger the rescued forgetteth no kindness, he gives thee
the dragon."

Kingly the gift to behold. The heavy curved planks of
oak timber

Matched not together like others, but grew in one broad
piece united.

It stretched its huge form in the sea like a dragon, its
stem proudly lifted,

A stately head high in the air. Its throat with red
gold was all blazing;

Sprinkled its belly with yellow and azure, and back of
the rudder,

Covered with scales of pure silver, its tail lashed the
waves in a circle.

Bordered with red were its inky black pinions. When
all unfolding,

It flew in a race with the whirlwind, and left far behind the swift eagle.

When it was filled with armed warriors, you'd fancy you
were beholding

A citadel swimming the billows, or palace o'er ocean
wave flying.

Widely renowned was that ship, and of ships was the
chief in the Northland.

All this and other vast treasures did Fridthjof receive
from his father.

Scarce was there found in the Northland any with richer
possessions,

Save were he heir of a kingdom, for of kings is the
wealth always greatest.

Though from no king he descended, yet was his mind
truly royal,

Courteous, noble and kind. Daily became he more
    famous.
Twelve gray-haired champions, valorous chieftains, sat at
    his table,
Thorstein's steel-breasted companions, whose brows were
    with scars deeply furrowed.
Next to the warriors was seated a youth of the same
    age as Fridthjof,—
Like a fresh rose 'mid the dry leaves of autumn; Bjorn
    was this blossom,—
Glad as a child, but firm as a man and wise as an old
    man.
Grown up with Fridthjof, in days of their boyhood their
    blood they commingled,
Brothers becoming in good northern fashion, sworn to
    each other
In joy and in grief, the survivor avenging the death of
    his comrade.

In the midst of the warriors and guests who had come
    to the funeral banquet,
Fridthjof, a sorrowing host, his eyelids with tears over-
    flowing,

Drank in accordance with ancestral usage, a skoal to
    his father,

Heard the old minstrels sing loudly his praises, a thun-
    dering drapa,

Rightfully took of his late father's seat undisputed pos-
    session,

And sat between Odin and Frey. So sitteth Thor up
    in Valhal.

IV.

FRIDTHJOF'S COURTSHIP.

L OUD sounded the music in Fridthjof's hall,
   His ancestors' praises sang poets all.
O'erwhelmed with sadness
Is Fridthjof, he hears not their songs of gladness.

The earth has again donned her mantle of green
And dragon-ships breasting the waves are seen ;
But Fridthjof, pondering,
Is at the moon gazing or in the woods wandering.

How fortunate was he but lately, and glad,
For Helge and Halfdan as guests he had ;
And with the brothers,
Came Ingeborg; Fridthjof scarce saw the others.

He sat by her side and her soft hand he pressed ;
He felt in the pressure returned him thrice blest,
Enraptured gazing
On her whom he honored beyond all praising.

In glad conversation recalling their plays,
When life's morning dew presaged bright future days,
For memory truthful
Keeps life's rosy gardens in noble minds youthful.

How fondly she greets him from dale and from park,
From loving names growing in white birchen bark,
From hills where flourish
The oaks which the ashes of heroes nourish.

" 'Tis never so pleasant at home as here,
For Halfdan is childish and Helge severe;
The kings attending
To nothing but prayers and praise unending.

"And no one (nor could she her blushes hide)
To whom my complainings I may confide.
The palace building,
How stifling compared with the groves of Hilding.

"The doves that we petted, and tamed and fed,
By hawks oft affrighted away have fled;
One pair remaineth,
Let Fridthjof take one, one Ing'borg retaineth.

"She'll long like another her friend to see,—

And homeward returning will fly to me:

Your message, bind it

Beneath her fleet pinion,—there none will find it."

All day they sat whispering side by side,

Nor ceased the low murmur at eventide;

So breathe in whispers

The zephyrs through lindens at twilight vespers.

But now she has gone, and his joy forsooth

Has gone with the maiden. The blood of youth

His cheek is mounting,

He silently sighs while the past recounting.

His grief at her absence he sent by the dove,

Which joyous set out with its message of love;

But oh! new sorrow,—

It stayed with its mate, nor returned on the morrow.

His conduct to Bjorn was displeasing; said he:

"What ails our young eagle, he seems to be

Like some shy sparrow,—

Has his breast or his pinion been pierced by an arrow?

"What wilt thou, Fridthjof? We have for need
The yellow bacon, and the good, brown mead;
And poets singing,
Their jubilant music forever ringing.

"The steeds impatiently stamp in the stalls,—
To the chase! to the chase! the falcon calls;
But Fridthjof retaineth
His gloom. He hunteth in clouds and complaineth.

"Ellide is restless upon the main,—
She frets and she chafes at her cable chain;
Lie still my treasure!
Our Fridthjof is peaceable. Strife is no pleasure.

"Who dies on his pallet, is dead indeed;
By the lance, as did Odin, we'll die, if need,—
And thus ensure us
A welcome to Hel, and heaven secure us."

Then Fridthjof unloos'd the dragon,—and proud,
With full swelling canvas, the waves she plowed,
And swiftly over
The bay to the palace she bore the lover.

The kings were at Bele's grave met that day,—
To administer justice and counsel weigh;
Fridthjof advances,—
His voice sounds afar like clashing lances.

"Ye kings, lovely Ing'borg, the people's pride,
I choose, from all women, to be my bride;
The king intended
Our lives thus united in one should be blended.

"He reared us together in Hilding's sight,—
As two forest saplings whose tops unite,—
A golden cover
Of lace bindeth Freyja the green tops over.

"My sire was a peasant, no earl nor king,—
Yet his memory will live while the poets sing;
In runic story
The grave-mounds are telling my ancestors' glory.

"I could easily win me a crown and land,
But choose to remain on my native strand;
In battle wielding
My sword for the king, and the peasant shielding.

"On king Bele's grave we are standing now,
He hears every word in the grave below,
With me he pleadeth,—
(A dead father's counsel a wise son heedeth.")

Then Helge uprose, and replied with scorn,
"Our sister was not for a peasant born,
To kings 'tis given
To strive for our Ingeborg, daughter of heaven.

"You boastfully call yourself chief of swords,—
Win men by violence, women by words;
Boast not of slaughter,
For arrogance winneth not Odin's daughter.

"My kingdom doth not seek protection from thee,
I shield it myself. My man wouldst thou be,—
A situation
Among my domestics befits thy station."

"Thy servant! no, never!" was Fridthjof's reply,
"My father had never a master,—shall I?
From thy silver dwelling
Now fly, Angervadil, the insult repelling."

In sunshine now glitters the blue steel blade,—
Displaying its letters in flaming red.
" My good sword loyal,
Thy lineage at least," said Fridthjof, " is royal.

"And were it not now for the high grave's renown,
Right here would I hew thee, swarthy king, down ;
Yet will I teach thee
To come not again where my sword can reach thee."

So saying, he severed at one fell blow
The gold shield of Helge which hung on a bough.
It fell asunder,—
Its clang on the grave-mound was echoed under.

" Well done, Angervadil! lie still and dream
Of high achievements,— meanwhile the gleam
Of rune-fires paling!
And now we'll go home o'er the blue waters sailing."

V.

KING RING.

KING RING moved his gold-stool back.   Then up-
    rose
    Champion and dreamer,—
For where in the North does such goodness repose?
His word o'erflows
    With the wisdom which dwells in god Mimer.

Like the groves of the peaceful gods was his land,—
    War's sable pinion
Cast not a shadow where on every hand
Flowers expand
    Through the length of his quiet dominion.

Here Justice alone on the judgment-seat
    With Right presided;
And Peace every year paid its tribute meet,—
While golden wheat
    With plenty the harvest provided.

And swarthy-prowed ships to this favored shore,
  With snowy pinions
The products of numberless nations bore,—
A varied store
  Of riches for fortune's rich minions.

Here freedom and peace did in concord dwell,
  Kindly united;
And all loved their father, the king, full well,
For each might tell
  His mind in the thing,*—none were slighted.

Supreme in the Northland through thirty years
  His reign extended;
Contented each went to his daily cares;
At evening prayers
  The king's name in blessings ascended.

King Ring moved his gold-stool back. From the board
  All there assembled
Arose to attend on the royal word,—
Renowned where heard;
  But he sighed, and in accents that trembled,

* See glossary.

He said: "My lost queen is in Folkvang-hall
  On purple seated;
But here on her grave is a grassy pall,
While breathe o'er all
  The flowers with sweet odor freighted.

"So queenly, so honored, so good and so fair,
  There's not another.
Immortal she dwelleth in Valhal's care,
But the people's prayer,
  The children's desire, is a mother.

"King Bele oft sat as a guest at my side
  When winter ended;
The daughter he left I would choose for my bride,—
Her father's pride,
  In whose cheeks rose and lily are blended.

"I know she is young, and in youth sublime
  Would gather flowers;
My flower is past and my early prime;
My locks has Time
  Besprinkled with snowy showers.

Oh, could she but honor the withered tree
   Which age has blighted;
And could she a friend to the motherless be,
Then should you see
   To the throne Spring by Autumn invited.

"Take gold from my coffers, take jewels rare,
   Unstinted measure;
Let minstrels attending the way prepare
To win the fair,—
   For song heralds wooing and pleasure."

With gold and petitions, a noisy throng,
   The young men speeded;
And minstrels and skalds, in procession long,
With hero-song
   To the sons of King Bele proceeded.

The feast, where with wassail they drink and sing,
   For three days lasted,   [bring
But they sought the fourth morning what answer they'd
From Helge king,—
   For now their return must be hasted.

In the grove Helge offered both bird and beast,—
    A sacred duty;
Asked counsel of vala, consulted the priest
What answer was best
    For the queen of affection and beauty.

The offerings and vala and priest denied
    The wished-for token;
And Helge, affrighted by signs he'd tried,
With "No," replied,
    For men must obey when the gods have spoken.

But merry king Halfdan laughed gayly, and said,
    "The feast is ended,
King Gray-beard himself should have come instead,
I'd glad have led
    His beast, and his mounting attended."

Indignant the embassy went away,
    Nor longer tarried;
"King Gray-beard his honor'll avenge one day,"
Is Ring heard to say,
    When to him the curt message is carried.

He strikes his bright shield hanging high on a bough,—

    His weapon seizes;

And many a dragon is hurrying now,

With blood-red prow, ·

    And helmet plumes wave in the breezes.

The tidings flew swiftly to Helge king,

    Who answered slowly:

"The strife will be bloody, for mighty is Ring;

My sister bring

    To the temple of Balder, the holy."

There sitteth the loving one, full of woes,

    Though safe abiding;

She weeps, while with silk and with gold she sews;

A tear o'erflows,—

    The dew 'mid the lilies is hiding.

VI.

FRIDTHJOF PLAYS CHESS.

BJORN and Fridthjof chess were playing
On a board, whose squares displaying
   Gold and silver deftly fitted,
     Skill and beauty both combined.
Then stepped Hilding in. "Come nigher,"
Fridthjof said, "and sit thee higher
   'Till our game shall be completed,—
     Come, my foster-father kind."

Hilding answered: "From the palace
I am come to you for solace.
   Evil are the times at present,
     You are all the people's hope."
Fridthjof said: "The foe encroaches,
Danger, Bjorn, your king approaches;
   You can save him by a peasant,—
     He is nothing, give him up."

"Fridthjof, anger kings no longer,
Lo, the eagle's young grow stronger;
Ring may thwart their weak endeavor,
Thou wilt surely find it hard."
"Bjorn, I see you storm the tower,
All in vain your threatening power
'Gainst the castle is; it ever
Safety seeks behind its guard."

"Ing'borg sits in Balder's dwelling,
Grief her constant tears compelling;
She should make thee seize thy armor
She with tearful eyes of blue."
"Vain you strive my queen to capture,
Dear from childhood's days of rapture;
Best of all, there's naught shall harm her —
Come what may, to her I'm true."

"Fridthjof, art thou still unheeding
All thy foster-father's pleading?
For thy foolish game art ready
I should go without a word?"

Fridthjof then arises, laying
Hilding's hand in his, and saying:
  "My resolve is firm and steady,
    And my answer you have heard.

  "Go to Bele's sons and warn them,
Peasants love not those who scorn them;
  To their power I bid defiance,
    Their behests will not obey."
  "In thy chosen way abide thee,
For thy wrath I can not chide thee;
  Odin must be our reliance,"
    Hilding said, and went his way.

VII.

FRIDTHJOF'S HAPPINESS.

KING Bele's sons may go requesting
   From dale to dale the peasants' aid,
In Balder's grove my world is resting,
   For them I will not draw my blade.
Then on king's vengeance or earth's sadness,
   I will no longer look or think,
But only will the high gods' gladness,
   From out one cup with Ing'borg drink.

While yet the hazy sunshine sendeth
   Its purple rays on flowers at rest,
Like rosy gossamer which lendeth
   An added charm to Ing'borg's breast,
With sighs along the strand I wander,
   My soul with longing all aflame,
Upon the sand I gaze and ponder
   And with my sword write Ing'borg's name.

How slowly go the lonesome hours!

    Thou Delling's son, why stayest thou?

Hast thou not seen our mountain bowers,

    Our lakes and islands until now?

Dwells there in western halls no maiden

    Who waits since morn first kissed the sea,

Upon thy breast her joys to unladen,

    Whose whole of life is love and thee?

At last thy footsteps grow uncertain,

    Thy weary journey thou must close,

Now evening draws the rosy curtain,

    Behind whose folds the gods repose.

The brooks and breezes to each other

    In softest whispers love express;

O! welcome Night, of gods the mother,

    With pearls upon thy wedding dress.

The stars are gliding like a lover

    On tiptoe to a maiden true;

Ellide! fly the deep gulf over,

    Roll on, roll on, ye billows blue.

Yon sacred grove a temple hideth,

   Good Balder's temple, doubly dear,

For there love's goddess safe abideth,

   Unto the gods our course we steer.

Thy shores I tread with joyous measure,

   I kiss thy brown cheek, smiling earth,

And all ye little flowers, with treasure

   Of white and red, that edge my path.

I hail thee, moon, with pale light streaming

   On temple-grove and flowers at rest,

How beautiful thou sittest dreaming

   Like Saga at a wedding feast.

To speak with flowers, O, brook, who taught thee

   The feeling in my heart a guest?

Ye northern nightingales, where caught ye

   The wailing stolen from my breast?

With evening's red the fairies playing,

   In clouds my Ing'borg's form disclose,

But Freyja, jealousy displaying,

   Away the image quickly blows.

Though changing clouds lose her resemblance,
  Like radiant hope herself appears,
As true as childhood's sweet remembrance,
  She comes, my love's reward she bears.
Come, loved one, come, and let me press thee,
  Unto the heart that holds thee dear,
My soul's desire, through life I'll bless thee,
  Come to my arms, and rest thee here.

Frail as the lily's stem so slender,
  Yet like spring roses fresh and fair,
As Freyja's troth-plight, warm and tender,
  Thou as the will of gods art pure.
Kiss me, and let my burning passion
  Kindle thy soul to perfect bliss,
Of earth and heaven I lose the vision,
  Enraptured by thy melting kiss.

Fear not, for here can come no stranger,
  Without stands Bjorn, his sword in hand,
His champions guarding us from danger,
  If need be, can the world withstand;

And I, if fighting for my treasure,
  Whose form I on my bosom bear,
To Valhal now would go with pleasure,
  Could'st thou be my valkyrie there.

And why fear Balder's fierce resentment,
  The pious god to whom we pray?
He looks on us with calm contentment,
  For, loving, we his law obey.
The god whose brow with sunshine beameth,
  With whom all truth abideth sure,
His love unto his Nanna seemeth,
  Like mine to thee, so warm, so pure.

There stands his image, not indignant,
  But mild and soft as sunset ray,
Upon this shrine of god benignant,
  My heart a sacrifice I lay.
Together let us kneel before him,
  No better offering can be found
Than two fond hearts which both adore him,
  With love like his together bound.

Scorn not my love, my blossom cherished,

  Which more to heaven than earth belongs,

In heaven itself that love was nourished,

  And for that glorious home it longs.

Oh! that my weary soul releasing,

  The gods would take me up above;

Triumphantly, with joy unceasing,

  I'd go, embraced by my dear love.

When bugle-notes the champions rally,

  From out the silver gates they ride;

But I alone join not the sally,

  I linger gladly by thy side.

When Valhal's maidens pass me, smiling,

  The mead-horn with its rim of gold;

Thee, only thee, my love beguiling,

  My tender, loving arms enfold.

A leafy cottage near the meadow

  I'd build us by the dark-blue sea,

And there we'd rest us 'neath the shadow

  Of many a golden-fruited tree;

And when bright Valhal's sun each morning,
    With his clear torch in splendor rose,—
We'd hasten to the gods returning,
    Yet longing for our home's repose.

Thy golden locks, with sunshine flushing,
    Wreathed with a starry crown should be;
So my pale lily, rosy blushing,
    In Vingolf-hall should dance with me.
Then, by my love from danger guarded,
    I'd with thee to our home repair,—
Where singeth Brage, silver-bearded,
    Our wedding song each evening fair.

How sweet the evening song-bird's vesper!
    It cometh forth from Valhal's shore;
How soft the moon-beams' gentle whisper,
    From where the dead live evermore!
They tell of light and love unbroken,
    In homes devoid of care and pain;
Where joyous words alone are spoken,
    There thou my love shalt ever reign.

Oh, weep not, love, those tears regretful,

    While through my heart the life-blood streams;

But sweetly sleep,— of grief forgetful

    May love and Fridthjof fill thy dreams.

Oh! when thine arms thou foldest round me,

    When thy dear eyes but look on me,

How quickly breaks the spell that bound me,

    How turn my thoughts from heaven to thee!

"List to the lark's melodious numbers."

    Nay, 'tis a dove his love-song sings,

The lark on yonder hillock slumbers,

    Beside his mate with folded wings.

How happy they, always together,

    As free their life as wings that bear

Through cheerless storm or sunny weather,

    Above the clouds, that happy pair.

"See, daybreak comes." Nay, but ascended

    From some far beacon is the light;

Our happy talk is not yet ended,

    Nor yet so soon the lovely night.

Bright morning star, sleep till to-morrow,

　And when night cometh, slumber still,

Your waking brings to Fridthjof sorrow,—

　So sleep till doomsday, if you will.

Vain hope! No longer earth reposes,

　The morning breeze new pleasure seeks;

Already bud the eastern roses,

　As fresh as those on Ing'borg's cheeks.

I hear the winged songsters twitter,

　A thoughtless throng in the opening sky;

All life's astir, the wavelets glitter,

　And lover must with shadows fly.

Ah! there he comes, in glory beaming;

　Forgive, O golden sun, my prayer.

How beautiful, in splendor gleaming!

　I feel—I know a god is near.

Oh! who could, in thy path advancing,

　With equal grace and power tread,

All hearts with light and joy entrancing,

　A life like thine victorious lead!

Here, 'neath thy watchful eye I leave her—
　　My peerless beauty of the North!
Let not the rough world's troubles grieve her,
　　Thy likeness on the green-clad earth.
Her soul is pure as rays of morning,
　　Her eyes as-blue as thine own sky,
The same rich tints thy crown adorning
　　Among her golden tresses lie.

Farewell, my love, be not forgetful,
　　Some longer night again we'll meet;
I, lingering, kiss thy brow, regretful,
　　One kiss I give thy lips so sweet.
Sleep now, beloved; in thy slumber,
　　May dreams of me thy bosom swell,
At mid-day wake, and with me number
　　Each absent hour; farewell, farewell.

VIn.

THE PARTING.

INGEBORG.

THE day breaks clear, and Fridthjof cometh not,
　Though yesterday the council was proclaimed
At Bele's grave.　The place was rightly chosen,
His daughter's fate should be determined there.
How many supplications hath it cost me,
How many tears by Freyja counted o'er,
To melt the ice of hate　round Fridthjof's heart,
And gain a promise from his haughty lips
To give his hand in reconciliation.
Alas! how hard is man!　And for his honor,
So calleth he his pride, he counts it not,
Or lightly counts it, if he rudely break,
Of true and faithful hearts one more or less.
But wretched woman, leaning on his breast,
Is like the moss-growth blooming on the cliff,—
With faded tints, it difficultly holds
Itself unnoticed fast unto the rock,

Is only nourished by the dews of night.

But yesterday, indeed, my fate was fixed,

And now the evening sun hath set upon it,

Still Fridthjof cometh not. The pallid stars

Die one by one, and sadly disappear,

And with each one of them a hope is quenched

And goes from out my heart unto its grave.

Ah! wherefore still to hope? Valhal's gods

No longer love me; I've offended them.

And Balder, 'neath whose shelter I reside,

Is wroth with me, because a human love

Is too unholy for the sight of gods,

And earthly joy must never risk itself

Beneath the temple-arch in which the grave,

The haughty powers have fixed their dwelling-place.

And yet what fault is mine? and wherefore frowns

The pious god upon a maiden's love?

Is it not pure as Urd's bright sparkling fount,

And innocent as Gefjon's morning dream?

The shining sun doth never turn away

From loving ones, its pure and watchful eyes.

And daylight's widow, starry night, doth hear

With gladness, in her sorrow, all their vows.

That which is worthy under heaven's vault,

Can that be guilty 'neath the temple's dome?

I love my Fridthjof. Oh! through all the past,

As far as memory runs, I loved him well,—

A holy feeling twin-born with my soul,

I know not whence it came, nor comprehend

The dismal thought that it was ever gone.

As fruit is timely set about the stone

And groweth up, and round about it all

In summer sunshine wraps its cloth of gold,

So, too, indeed, have I maturing grown

About this stone, and my existence is

Of my affection but the outer shell.

Forgive me, Balder! With a faithful heart

Thy hall I sought, and with a faithful one

Will I go hence; I'll take it with me now

Out over Bifrost-bridge, and place myself

With all my love before great Valhal's gods.

And there my love, like them an Asa-child,

Shall see itself reflected in the shields,

And fly with loosened dove-wings through the blue

Unending space unto the Allfather's bosom,

From whence it came. Oh! wherefore is the frown,

In morning's twilight, on thy brow so fair?

There floweth in my veins, as flows in thine,

Old Odin's blood. What wilt thou, kinsman dear?

My ardent love I cannot offer thee,

Nor would I offer it, worth all thy joys;

But I can offer thee my life's delight,—

Can cast it from me as the stately queen

Her mantle flings aside, and still remains

Her queenly self. But my resolve is taken,

And Valhal high shall never be ashamed

To own me kindred. I will meet my fate

As meets the hero his. Ah! here he comes!

How wild he seems, how pale! 'Tis done, 'tis done!

My angry norn she comes beside him now;

Be strong, my soul! At last I welcome thee.

Our fate is fixed; 'tis plain to read it where

Upon thy brow it stands.

FRIDTHJOF.

And stand not there

As well, the blood-red runes, which speak of shame,

And scorn and banishment?

6

INGEBORG.

Oh, Fridthjof, think!
Relate what passed, for I have long foreseen
The worst, and am prepared for all.

FRIDTHJOF.

I found the council at our fathers' graves.
Around the grassy mounds, shield meeting shield,
Stood many Northland sons with swords in hand,
One circle standing close within another
Unto the top. Upon the judgment seat,
A thunder cloud, thy brother Helge sat,—
A pallid headsman with a dusky look.
And next to him, a seeming grown up child,
Sat Halfdan,—thoughtless, playing with his sword.
Then I arose, and said: "War waiting stands
Within thy borders, beating on the shield,—
Thy kingdom now, king Helge, is in peril;
Give me thy sister, and I'll give to thee
Mine arm, it may be useful in this strife.
Between us let ill will forgotten be,—
I would not cherish it 'gainst Ing'borg's brother.

To reason listen, king, and save at once
Thy golden crown, thy purest sister's heart.
Here is my hand. By Asa-Thor, I swear,
I'll never offer it again to thee."
An uproar shook the thing. A thousand swords
Approval hammered on a thousand shields.
The clang of weapons flew to heaven, which heard
With joy the assent of freemen to the right.
"To him give Ingeborg, the slender lily,
Most beautiful our dales have ever grown;
No better sword our favored land can boast,—
To him give Ingeborg." Our foster-father,
The reverend Hilding, with his silver-beard,
Stood forth and spoke in words of wisdom full,
Short apothegms, as keen as sharpened swords.
And Halfdan, too, from off the royal seat
Arose, with pleading words and pleading looks,—
But it was all in vain; each prayer was wasted,—
Like sunshine lavished on a barren rock,
No growth alluring from his stony heart.
King Helge's sullen countenance was like
His heart,—a pale-faced "No" to human prayers.
"A peasant's son," said he, contemptuously,

"Could Ing'borg gain, but who profanes the temple

Ill-suited seems to holy Valhal's daughter.

Hast thou not, Fridthjof, broken Balder's peace?

Hast thou not seen my sister in his temple

When day had hid itself from your communion?

Say yes, or no!" A deafening shout resounded

From all those rings of men: "Say no, say no,

We take thee at thy word, we sue for thee,—

Thou son of Thorstein, equal to a king;

Say no, say no, and Ingeborg is thine!"

"My life's delight hangs on a feeble word,"

Said I, "but fear it not, king Helge!

I would not lie myself to Valhal's joy,

Much less to earth's. Thy sister I have seen,

Have talked with her beneath the temple's night,

But Balder's peace I have not therefore broken."

They let me say no more. Abhorrent cries

Flew through the thing, and those who nearest stood

Drew back as from a pestilent disease;

And when I looked around, their superstition

Had palsied every tongue, and blanched each cheek

So lately glowing with expectant joy.

And then king Helge triumphed. With a voice

As sad, as awful as the ghostly vala's
In Vegtam's song, when she for Odin sung
Of asas' fate and grim Hel's victory,
So sad he spoke: "Though banishment or death
I could decree, by our ancestral laws
Against this crime, yet I'll be mild as Balder,
Whose sacred dwelling thou hast so profaned.
The western sea a wreath of islands holds,   .
Where Angantyr, the earl, is governor.
As long as Bele lived the earl each year
His tribute paid, but ceased when Bele died.
Go o'er the sea and drive this tribute in;
This penance thy audacity demands.
'Tis said," sneered he, with meanest mockery,
"That Angantyr hard-fisted is, and broods
Like dragon Fafner o'er his gold; but who
Can stand 'gainst our new Sigurd, Fafner's bane?
Exploits more manly must thou undertake
Than luring maidens under Balder's roof.
·When summer comes shall we expect you here
With all thy honor, first of all the tribute.
If not, thou art to every man a felon,

And during life art outlawed through the land."

His judgment rendered, he dissolved the thing.

INGEBORG.

And your decision?

FRIDTHJOF.

Have I aught to choose?

Is not mine honor bound by his decree?

And that will I redeem though Angantyr

His paltry gold doth hide in Nastrand's flood.

To-day will I depart.

INGEBORG.

And Ing'borg leave?

FRIDTHJOF.

Nay, nay, I leave thee not, thou goest too.

INGEBORG.

Impossible!

FRIDTHJOF.

O! hear me, ere thou answerest.

Thy crafty brother seemeth to forget,

That Angantyr was my dear father's friend,

As well as Bele's. Perhaps he'll give

Without constraint what I demand; if not

A worthy advocate, a sharp one too,

Have I. 'Tis always ready at my side.

The gold he covets I'll to Helge send,

And thus will I from sacrificial knife

Of this crowned hypocrite redeem us both.

But we, my beauteous Ingeborg, will spread

O'er seas unknown Ellide's willing sail,—

She'll kindly bear us to a friendlier strand

Where exiled love may safe asylum find.

What is the North to me? And what a race,

Which pales at every word of priest or king,

Whose shameless hands would pluck the living rose

From out the sanctuary of my heart?

So, Freyja help, it shall not prosper them!

The wretched slave is bound unto the turf

Where he was born, but I will still be free,

Free as the mountain winds. A little earth

From Bele's grave and from my father's taken,

Can find a place upon our ship, and that

Is all of fatherland that we can need.

My loved one, there another sun is found

Than that which pales above these hills of snow,

And there another sky, more bright than this;

And milder stars with god-like glance adorned,

Look down therefrom in balmy summer nights

On lovers wandering in the laurel groves.

My father, Thorstein, Viking's son, in wars

Had journeyed far, and oft I've heard him tell,

By fireside light in winter evenings long,

About the Grecian sea with islands filled,—

Fresh groves of green in brightly shining waves.

A powerful race once had its dwelling there,—

And holy gods the marble temples graced.

But now they stand deserted; grasses thrive

In paths left desolate, and flowers grow

From out the runes that tell of ancient lore;

The slender columns stand like budding trees

Entwined by graceful stems of southern vines.

Throughout the year the earth spontaneous yields,

In unsown harvests, all that men require.

There golden apples glow between the leaves,

And blushing grapes from every bough hang down

And, ripening, swell luxurious as thy lips.

There, Ing'borg, there we'll build us near the wave

A little North, more beautiful than this;

And with our ever faithful love we'll fill

The radiant temple vaults, and thus delight

With human fondness the forgotten gods.

And when, with loosened sheets (no storms are there)

The sailor idly floats along our isle

In twilight's glow, and turns his joyous glance

From rosy-colored ripples to the strand,—

Upon the temple's threshold shall he see

A second Freyja, Aphrodite called

In southern tongue, and he shall wonder at

The golden locks, seen flowing in the breeze,

And eyes which brighter gleam than southern skies.

And one by one around her groweth up

A little temple-dwelling race of fairies,

With cheeks where you might see the south had set,

In Northern snowdrifts, freshly blooming roses.

Ah! Ingeborg, how beautiful, how near,

Stands earthly happiness to faithful hearts;

If they are brave enough to seize it when disposed,

It follows willingly, and builds for them

A Vingolf even here beneath the clouds.

7

O come, let's haste away, each spoken word

A moment shorter makes our waiting joy.

Come, all's prepared! Ellide stretches now

Her shadowy eagle wings for eager flight,—

And freshly blowing winds now guide the way

Henceforth from this inconstant land forever.

Why tarriest thou?

INGEBORG.

I cannot follow thee.

FRIDTHJOF.

Not follow me?

INGEBORG.

Ah! Fridthjof, thou art blest!

Thou followest none, but always in the front,—

The stem of thy good dragon ship, dost place

Thy will beside the helm, to steer the way .

With steady hand above the wrathful waves.

How widely different the case with me!

My cruel fate is held in other's hands,

Which loosen not the prey although it bleed;

And sacrifice, lament and lonesome pining,
Is all king Bele's daughter knows of freedom.

FRIDTHJOF.

Art thou not free, if so thou willest?   In the grave
Thy father sits.

INGEBORG.

No, Helge is my father,
Is in my father's stead; on his consent
My hand depends, and Ing'borg will not steal
Her happiness, however near it stands.
Ah! what would woman be if she cut loose
The sacred band with which the Allfather binds
Unto the stronger power her gentle being?
The water-lily pale resembles her;
It rises with the wave and with it falls,
The sailor's keel goes forward over it
And marks it not although it cut the stem.
Such is indeed her fate! And yet the flower,
As long as clings the root unto the sand,
Its growth increases, borrowing color pure
From its pale sister stars which shine above,—
Itself a star upon the waters blue.

But rudely broken loose, it ceaseless drives,

A withered leaf along deserted waves.

Last night,— that was indeed a fearful night,

An unrewarded watch I kept for thee,

And children of the night, the serious thoughts,

With raven locks went thronging closely by

My ever watchful, burning, tearful eyes;

And Balder, too, the bloodless god looked down

On me with frowning glances full of threats.

Last night I pondered o'er my wretched fate.

My resolution's taken; I remain

Obedient victim at my brother's altar.

Yet it is well I did not hear thee then,

With fabled islands floating in the clouds

Where evening's glowing twilights always show

A flowery world of peace and happy love.

Who knows how weak one is? My childhood dreams

Though silent long, with joy rise up again,

And whisper in my anxious ear with voice

Familiar as a sister's kindly tones,

As tender as a lover's ardent praise.

I hear ye not! ah, no, I hear ye not,

Alluring accents once so fondly loved!

A child of Northland cannot elsewhere dwell;

Too pale am I for those bright summer roses;—

Too colorless my mind for that deep glow;

The scorching sun would quite consume me there.

Of anxious longing full, my eyes would seek

The northern star which always watchful stands

A heavenly sentry o'er our fathers' graves.

My noble Fridthjof shall not now desert

The cherished land that he was born to guard;

He shall not fling away his honored name

To gain so poor a thing, a maiden's love.

A life where spins the sun from year to year,

And where each day is ever like the next —

A beauteous but unending sameness, is

For woman only, but for manly souls,

And most for thine, it's quiet, weary dullness.

Thou thrivest best where storms are raging round.

On foaming pacers o'er the heaving sea,

And on thy tossing plank, come life or death,

Thou mayest fight with peril for thine honor.

The beauteous desert thou dost paint, would be

A grave for high achievements, not yet born;

And like thy shield, with rust would be dissolved,

Thine independent mind. It shall not be!

I will not steal away my Fridthjof's name

From poet's storied song; I will not quench

My hero's glory in its morning dawn.

Be wise, my Fridthjof; let us yield unto

The haughty norn; let us rescue yet

Our cherished honor from this wreck of life;

Our happiness we cannot save, 'tis gone,

And separate we must!

FRIDTHJOF.

And wherefore must?

Because a sleepless night disturbed thy mind?

INGEBORG.

Because my honor must be saved, and thine.

FRIDTHJOF.

A woman's honor rests on manly love.

INGEBORG.

Not long loves he whom he cannot respect.

FRIDTHJOF.

Respect is not by fickle fancy gained.

INGEBORG.

A sense of justice is a noble fancy.

FRIDTHJOF.

Our love strove not with justice yesterday.

INGEBORG.

Nor love to-day, but all the more our flight.

FRIDTHJOF.

Necessity commands our flight,— Oh, come!

INGEBORG.

What's right and noble, that's necessity.

FRIDTHJOF.

High rides the sun and time is fleeting by.

INGEBORG.

Ah, me, it has gone by, gone by forever!

FRIDTHJOF.

Consider well. Is that thy last resolve?

INGEBORG.

I have considered well; it is my last.

FRIDTHJOF.

Farewell then, fare thee well, king Helge's sister.

INGEBORG.

Oh, Fridthjof! Fridthjof! must we separate thus?

Hast thou indeed no friendly glance to give

Thy childhood's friend; no kindly hand to reach

To the unfortunate, once so beloved?

Think'st thou I stand on roses here, and turn

Away with smiles my happiness for life?

And that I pangless tear from out my breast

A hope that hath with my affections grown?

Oh! wert thou not my heart's own morning dream?

Each joy that I have known was Fridthjof named,

And all of life that great or noble seemed,

Did Fridthjof's likeness take before mine eyes.

Bedim the image not: oh, do not meet

With cruelty the weak one offering up

The dearest thing upon the face of earth,

The dearest thing that Valhal's gods can give!

That offering, Fridthjof, is severe enough,

And words of consolation well deserves.

I know thou lovest me — that I have known

E'er since my being first began to dawn;

And Ing'borg's thoughts will surely follow thee

For years to come wherever thou may'st go.

The clang of warlike weapons deadens grief.

'Tis blown away upon the wild, wild waves,

Nor ventures to return when champions all

Their victory celebrate with drinking horn.

Yet sometimes, then, when in the peace of night,

Thy thoughts review again forgotten days,

There will among them glide an image pale,

Thou knowest well; it fondly greeteth thee

From regions dear; it is the image of

The virgin pale in Balder's holy grove.

Thou must not drive it thence away, although

It looketh sorrowful, but whisper kind

Into its ear a friendly word; the winds

Of night on faithful wings will bear it me;

One comfort yet, I have none else beside.

For me there's naught to dissipate my grief;

In all surrounding me it hath a tongue;

The holy temple vaults speak but of thee;

The temple's God, which should all threatening seem,

Thy likeness takes when shines the streaming moon.

Behold the sea — there swam thy keel through foam
To her who on the strand awaited thee;
Behold the woods — there stand so many stems
With Ing'borg's runes engraven in the bark;
Now grows the bark and wears away my name,
And that betokens death, the sagas say.
I ask the day when last it saw thy form,
I ask the night, but both are silent still;
And e'en the sea which bears thee, gives reply
But with a solemn sigh along the shore.
With evening's ruddy glow I'll send to thee
A greeting, when it sinks into thy waves.
And heaven's long ship, the fleeting cloud, shall take
On board the wail of the abandoned one.
So shall I sit within my virgin bower,
In mourning clad, of all life's joy bereft,
And broken lilies sew into the cloth,
Until the Spring its cloth doth weave, and sew
It full of better lilies on my grave.
And when I sadly take the harp to sing
Unending sorrow in profoundest tones,
Then burst the burning tears as now —

FRIDTHJOF.

Thou conquerest, Bele's daughter, weep no more!

Forgive my wrath, it was alone my sorrow

Which for a moment took a wrathful dress,—

A wrathful dress it cannot long endure.

Thou art my kindest norn, my Ingeborg.

(A noble mind best teaches what is noble.)

Necessity's real wisdom cannot have

A fairer, better advocate than thou,

Thou beauteous vala with the rosy lips!

I yield indeed unto necessity;

I part with thee but part not with my hope;

I'll take it with me over western waves,

I'll take it with me to the gates of death.

The nearest spring-day sees me here again;

King Helge, so I hope, shall see me too.

Then from my promise freed, his bidding done,

The calumny against me, too, atoned,

Then I'll request thee,— nay but I'll demand

In open council and with naked swords,

And not of Helge but of Northland's sons,

Who only can dispose a princess' hand;

I have a word for him who dare refuse.

Farewell till then; be true, forget me not,

And take, in memory of our childhood's love,

My arm-ring here, a beauteous Volund-work,

With heaven's wonders graven in the gold;

(The best of wonders is a faithful heart.)

How well it suits thine arm so snowy-white —

A glow-worm coiled around the lily's stem!

Farewell, my bride, my loved one, fare thee well.

Ere many moons our mournful lot will change.

                          [*He goes.*]

           INGEBORG.

How glad, how trusting, and of hope how full!

He sets the glittering point of his good sword

Against the norns, and says: "Ye must retreat!"

Thou wretched Fridthjof, the norns will ne'er retreat;

They go their way and laugh at Angervadil.

How little knowest thou my gloomy brother.

Thy brave, heroic temper fathoms not

The awful depths of his, nor understands

The hate that in his envious bosom burns.

His sister's hand he'll never give to thee;

He'd sooner give his crown, pour out his life,

Of me an offering make to Odin old,

Or to old Ring, whom now he fights against.

Wherever I may look, no hope is found,—

Yet am I glad hope lives within thy breast.

In secret will I keep my poor heart's wound,

And pray that all the good gods follow thee.

Here on thine arm-ring can I reckon up

Each separate month of all this lonesome sorrow.

In two, four, six,— then can'st thou come again,

But can'st not find again thine Ingeborg.

IX.

INGEBORG'S LAMENT.

A UTUMN has come;
Storming now heaveth the deep sea with foam,
Yet would I gratefully lie there,
Willingly die there.

Long gleamed his sail,
Flying to westward before the fierce gale;
Fortunate, Fridthjof to follow
O'er the wild billow.

Swell not so high,
Billows of blue with your deafening cry!
Stars lend assistance, a shining
Pathway defining.

With the spring doves
Fridthjof will come, but the maiden he loves
Cannot in hall or dell meet him,
Lovingly greet him.

Buried she sleeps,
Dead for her love's sake, or bleeding she weeps,
Heart-broken, given by her brother
Unto another.

Falcon he left,
Mine shalt thou be, winged hunter bereft;
I for thy owner will heed thee,
Lovingly feed thee.

Here on his hand,
'Broidering I'll picture thee on the cloth's rand,
Silvery pinions I'll give thee,
Golden claws weave thee.

Once, it is said,
Freyja with falcon-wings north and south sped,
Seeking for Oder, her lover,
All the world over.

Vainly I seek
Wings of the falcon, for mortals too weak;
Only in passing death's portal
Soareth a mortal.

Sit here with me,

Beautiful hunter and look at the sea;—

Longing and looking forever

Bringeth him never.

Dead shall I be,

When Fridthjof comes again over the sea;

Bear thou my love for his weeping,

I shall be sleeping.

X.

FRIDTHJOF AT SEA.

ON shore king Helge stood,
  By turns he sang and prayed,
And in embittered mood
  Besought the goblins' aid.

See! the heavens with darkness toiling,
  Empty space with thunders boom,
Lo, the furious waves are boiling,
  Ocean's surface hid with foam.
Lightnings now the clouds are streaking,
  Here and there a bloody rand,
All the sea-fowls now are shrieking,
  Hasting to the safer strand.

  "Hard's the weather, brothers!
  Hear the stormy pinions
  Flapping in the distance,
  Yet we do not pale.
8

Sit within the temple,
Think on me with longing,
Beauteous in thy weeping,
Beauteous Ingeborg."

———

'Gainst Ellide's stem,
    Two goblins warfare made.
One was wind-cold Ham,
    One was snowy Heyd.

Now the storm-wind wildly drifts them
    O'er the deep, and madly down;
Now it beating, whirling lifts them,
    Upward where the heavens frown.
All the powers of evil coming,
    Riding on the billows' top,
From the bottomless, the foaming,
    From the wide graves up.

    " Brighter was the journey
    By the pale moon's glimmer,
    Over mirrored waters
    Unto Balder's grove;

Warmer was it, nearer
Ing'borg's heart reposing;
Whiter than the sea-foam
Swelled her bosom fair."

———

Solund island fair
    Above the waves so white!
Stiller seas are there,
    Harbors safe invite.

But the bold sea-rover feareth
    Less upon the trusted oak,
Mans the helm himself, and jeereth
    At the wild wind's sportive stroke.
Tighter now the sail he fastens,
    Fleeter o'er the water skims,
Straight to westward fearless hastens,
    Goes where'er the billow swims.

"Fighting for a moment
With the storm delighteth;
Storm and Northman prosper
Well upon the wave.

Ingeborg would redden
Should her sea-eagle fly with
Slackened wings, affrighted
By a passing breeze."

Higher rise the waves,
 Deeper furrows plow,
Cordage madly raves,
 Creak both keel and prow.

Waves whichever way contending,
 With or 'gainst Ellide's form,
Meet good timbered sides, defending
 Menaced ship, defying storm.
Like an evening meteor sweeping,
 Joyful glides she through the night,
Like an Alpine roebuck leaping
 Over precipice and height.

"Better was it kissing
Her in Balder's temple,
Than to stand here tasting
Salt-foam as it whirls.

Better 'twas embracing
Bele's royal daughter
Than to stand here gripping
Fast the rudder's helm."

From the cold sky's field
   Snows intense prevail,
And on deck and shield
   Rattling storms of hail.

Lo, o'er all the vessel flying
   Night has placed her sable pall,
As in rooms where dead are lying,
   Gloomy darkness covers all.
Wave implacable now lashes
   Toward his doom the sailor brave,
White-gray as with sifted ashes
   Frightful yawns a boundless grave.

"Pillows Ran is making,
Luring us to quiet;
Thine I know are waiting,
Ingeborg, for me.

Faithful men are plying
Oars of good Ellide;
Gods the keel have made us,
Bear us yet awhile."

———

See the sea advance,
    Seeking now a wreck,
Ere the eye can glance,
    Clears the starboard deck.

Fridthjof's sinewy arm adorning,
    Shone a massive golden ring,
Bright as rays of early morning,
    'Twas the gift of Bele, king.
This in many pieces broken,—
    Made by dwarfs with skillful art,—
Gives to all on board a token,
    Every man receives a part.

"Gold is good to carry
When you go a-wooing,
Empty-handed no one
Comes to sea-blue Ran.

Cold is she to kisses,
Fleëth from embraces,
But the sea-bride yieldeth
Met with shining gold."

———

Now with threatenings new
    Falls the frozen storm,
Rends his sail in two,
    Snaps the brittle arm.

O'er Ellide's side prevailing
    Entering rolls the mountain wave,
Men of giant strength are baling,
    'Gainst the sea make battle brave.
Fridthjof cannot fail discerning
    That he carries death on board;
Then above the billows storming
    Rises his commanding word.

"Bjorn, attend the rudder,
Grip it with a bear's paw;
Valhal's holy powers
Never sent such storm.

Goblins rule the voyage;
Coward Helge chanted
Safety o'er the waters;
I will up and see."

Like a bird he flew
Up the icy spar,
Sat on high to view
Fiendish goblins war.

See, before Ellide gliding,
Like an island floating free,
Sea-whale on whose back are riding,
Loathsome goblins of the sea.
Heyd a snowy pelt doth cover,
Figure like a polar bear;
Ham hath wings which, waving hover
Eagle-like in stormy air.

"Now, Ellide, ready!
Show if hero temper
Dwells within your banded
Convex breast of oak.

Listen to my order;
Are you Valhal's daughter?
Strike with keel of copper,
Gore the conjured whale!"

Brave Ellide hears
    Fridthjof's proud behest.
With a spring she rears
    'Gainst the monster's breast.

From the wound a stream is driving,
    To the skies 'tis quickly sped,
Now the wounded monster diving,
    Roaring seeks his miry bed.
Fridthjof's giant strength then casteth
    Lances at the goblins bold,
One in Ice-bear's bosom fasteneth,
    One Storm-eagle's breast doth hold.

"Bravely done, Ellide!
Not so quickly riseth
Helge's magic dragon
Up from out the mire.

9

Ham and Heyd no longer
Rule the sea together;
Bitter is it biting
'Gainst the dark-blue steel."

———

Quickly disappears
   Storm from sea and land,
Gentle wavelet steers
   Toward the nearing strand.

All at once the sun advances,
   Like a king doth he unveil,
All enlivens, all entrances,
   Ship and billow, mount and dale.
Last rays, gleaming now like amber,
   Tops of cliff and forest bound,
Now each sailor well remembers
   The emerald shores of Efje Sound.

  "Ingeborg, pale maiden,
  Prayers sent unto Valhal;
  Lily-white she bowed her
  Knees on sacred gold.

Light-blue eyes in weeping,
Breast of swan's down, sighing,
Moved the hearts of asas;
Let us give them thanks."

———

Now Ellide leaks,
　Faithful dragon ship,
Shallow water seeks,—
　. Wearied of the trip.

Still more tired by labor dreary,
　Fridthjof's men desire the land;
But enfeebled, faint and weary,
　Sword-supported, scarce can stand.
Bjorn, on powerful shoulders, beareth
　Four of them and safely lands;
Fridthjof, too, the labor shareth,
　Eight sets round the burning brands.

"Do not blush, pale heroes!
Waves are sturdy vikings;
Hard indeed is fighting
'Gainst the ocean's bride.

See, there comes the mead-horn,
Gold the feet that bear it,
Warm your frozen members;
Skoal to Ingeborg!"

XI.

FRIDTHJOF WITH ANGANTYR.

'TIS now to tell the story
    How in his fir-wood hall,
Sat Angantyr, the hoary,
    And drank with champions all.
He, jóyous and light-hearted,
    Looked out to where the sun
Behind the waves departed,
    Just like a golden swan.

Outside the hall's commotion
    Old Halvard watched,— indeed
Not only watched the ocean,
    But also watched his mead.
His custom, seldom broken,
    Was, quick the horn to drain,
And ere a word was spoken,
    To thrust it in again.

But now he threw it; striding

   Into the hall he spake:

"I see the billows riding

   A ship, whose timbers shake;

I see some sailors dying

   Already on the strand,

And two strong giants, trying

   To bring the rest to land."

O'er waves no longer foaming,

   The noble earl looked out:

"That is Ellide coming,

   And Fridthjof too, no doubt;

His step, so firm and steady,

   Bespeaks him Thorstein's son;

Such brow, and smile so ready,

   In Northland there is none."

Then viking Atle sturdy

   Sprang up at one swift bound,

Black-bearded berserk, bloody,

   And fiercely looked around.

"Now, I will prove," he thunders,
     "What rumor means by this,
That all blades Fridthjof sunders,
     And never sues for peace."

And with the doughty viking,
     His twelve best champions start,
And in the air sharp striking,
     They brandish sword and dart.
They storm the strand, where by it
     The weary dragon lay;
But Fridthjof, sitting nigh it,
     Looks ready for the fray.

"Quite easy could I fell thee,"
     The noisy Atle cries;
"No one comes here, I tell thee,
     But either fights or flies.
If peace thou ask'st, believe me,—
     I fight, but am no churl,—
In friendship I'll receive thee,
     And lead thee to the earl."

"Although I'm scarcely rested,"
Is Fridthjof's sharp reply,
"Our good swords must be tested,
Before for peace I cry."
Then swift the sun-brown fighter
His flashing sword-blade swung,
Bright glowed the runes and brighter
On Angervadil's tongue.

Blows fell without cessation,
Now deadly blows like rain,
And now in quick rotation
Each shield is cleft in twain.
Unhurt, with wrath unspoken
They stand within the ring,—
Now Atle's sword is broken
And Fridthjof's sword is king.

Said he: "A swordless foeman
I've no desire to slay;
But if you will, as yeomen,
We'll try another way."

As waves 'gainst waves are pushing,
  And breaking crest on crest,
So on each other rushing,
  They wrestled breast to breast.

They fought like two bears trying
  Their strength on crust of snow,
Or, as o'er mad waves flying
  The eagle meets his foe.
The firm earth trembled round them,
  Though based on solid rock,
And oaks, though strong roots bound them,
  Could scarce withstand the shock.

Their brows with sweat were beaded,
  Their breasts heaved with a sound,
The brush and stones unheeded,
  They scattered all around.
The twelve in expectation
  Stood quaking on the sand;
Renowned through every nation
  That struggle on the strand.

But Fridthjof was the stronger,

   He felled his foe at last,

And said with fiery anger,

   His knee on Atle's breast:

"Had I my good sword ready,

   Thou berserk blackbeard, now

Thy miserable body

   I'd straightway plunge it through."

"Go bring it! Who'll prevent thee?"

   Is generous Atle's cry,

"And if it will content thee,

   As now I'll quiet lie.

Why should it make me sorrow?

   For all must Valhal see;

I go to-day — to-morrow

   Perhaps thy turn will be."

Then Fridthjof quick returning,

   Desired to end the fray;

Raised Angervadil burning,—

   But Atle quiet lay.

The falling blade ne'er harmed him,
 For Fridthjof struck the sand;
Such courage had disarmed him,
 He took brave Atle's hand.

With gleeful admonition
 Old Halvard swung his staff:
"For your battle-meal potation
 There's nothing here to quaff;
Upon the board hot-smoking
 The silver dishes glow;
A cold meal is provoking,
 And thirst annoys me so."

Appeased, with friendly feeling,
 The portals they pass through,
And here from floor to ceiling,
 To Fridthjof all was new.
Rough planks well matched together
 Lined not the spacious hall,
But 'broidered golden leather
 Was stretched along the wall.

The center was not littered
  By mortared hearthstone wide;
A marble fireplace glittered,
  Built up against the side.
No smoke 'mid rafters flitted,
  No roof with soot spread o'er;
Glass panes the windows fitted,
  A lock secured the door.

No wooden torches crackling,
  Illumed the champions' feast,
But waxen candles, sparkling, ˙
  In silver sconces placed.
A roasted stag, well larded,
  The table's center graced;
Gold bands his raised hoof guarded,
  With flowers his horns were dressed.

Beside each champion sitting,
  A youthful maiden stood,—
An evening star, bright flitting,
  Behind a stormy cloud;

The blue eyes beamed, in showers
  The gold-brown tresses flowed,
Complete as sculptured flowers
  The little rose-lips glowed.

On silver stool, high mounted,
  Sat Angantyr, the old;
His helm shot rays uncounted,
  His corselet was of gold.
His mantle, rich and splendid,
  With golden stars was strewn,—
And where the purple ended,
  The spotless ermine shone.

Three steps the earl descended;
  To Fridthjof genially
He said, with hand extended:
  "Come higher, sit by me.
Of horns I've emptied many
  With Thorstein in his day;
His son, more famed than any,
  Shall not sit far away."

He filled each goblet brimming
  With wine from Sicily,—
Like sparks of fire 'twas gleaming,
  And foaming like the sea.
"Welcome!" exclaimed the speaker,
  "My friend's most worthy son!
To Thorstein fill a beaker,—
  And drink now, every one!"

Now woke the harpstring's slumbers,
  A skald from Morven's hills,
In Gaul's melodious numbers,
  Sad hero-songs he trills.
But Thorstein's praise was chanted
  In old Norwayan tongue;
His noble deeds were vaunted,
  His daring valor sung.

The earl asked much concerning
  His friends of days gone by;
In words replete with learning
  Young Fridthjof made reply.

A judgment given blindly,
　　Swift accusation brings,
He spoke like Saga, kindly,
　　Remembering holy things.

And when he there recounted
　　How Helge goblins sent,
Which first the blue waves mounted,
　　Then, conquered, downward went,
The champions cheered him loudly,
　　And Angantyr the same,—
In high approval, proudly,
　　They echoed Fridthjof's name.

But when he spoke in anguish,
　　Of Ing'borg in her bloom,
How she was left to languish,
　　Her heart with grief o'ercome,—
Each maiden's cheek was burning,
　　Each bosom sore distressed;
And to her lover turning,
　　His faithful hand she pressed.

His embassy to mention
He ventured by and by;
The earl gave pleased attention,
And then he made reply:
" I ne'er was tributary;
King Bele's health, maybe,
To drink was customary,
But from his law we're free.

"His sons, I do not know them;
If tribute they demand,
Custom the way will show them,
We'll meet them on the strand,
And see who best is reckoned;
But Thorstein was my friend."
His daughter then he beckoned,
Who sat quite near at hand.

Then rose the maiden tender,
From stool all golden bound,
Her waist is trim and slender,
Her bosom full and round,

Each dimpled cheek encloses
    An Astrild, roguish sprite,
As when on opening roses,
    The butterflies alight.

She hastened to her bower,
    A green silk purse she brought,
With bird and tree and flower
    And beast 'twas deftly wrought;
On seas were white-winged vessels,
    Beneath the silver moon,
Of gold were all the tassels,
    The clasp with rubies shone.

She placed the dainty treasure
    Within her father's hand;
He filled it, brimming measure,
    With coin from foreign land.
"This welcome gift is only
    A tribute to a friend;
And now the winter lonely
    Consent with us to spend.
10

True courage knows no danger,
　　But Heyd and Ham, I fear,
Revived await the ranger,
　　And winter storms are here.
All foes the deep is hiding,
　　Ellide may not shun,
And many whales are riding
　　The waves, though conquered one."

With jesting and potation
　　The hours till day were spent,
Without inebriation
　　The wine-cup gladness lent.
A brimming skoal was given
　　To Angantyr at last;
So Fridthjof in this haven
　　The cheerful winter passed.

XII.

THE RETURN.

NOW spring is breathing in skies of blue,
   And earth her carpet has wove anew,
And Fridthjof grateful his kind host leaving
Again the billowy plain is cleaving,
And gayly speeding through silver-spray,
His black swan ploweth her sunny way.
The western breezes that spring is bringing,
Like nightingales in the sails are singing,
And Æger's daughters in veils of blue
About the rudder their sports pursue.
Ah, how delightful when safely clearing
A foreign land, to be homeward steering!
When memory pictures the smoke that curled
Above one's hearthstone, his childhood's world,
The fount where playing his swift feet hurried,
The honored graves where his dead are buried.
He thinks of her who perchance may be
On high cliffs standing to watch the sea.

Six days he sailed on his way returning,

The seventh a strip of blue discerning

Low down the horizon, he neared it fast,

Saw rock and islet and land at last.

That land is his; from the waves advancing,

He sees green forests in sunlight dancing.

He hears the roar of the foaming streams,

Can trace each cliff which with granite gleams,

Salutes the headland and sound, then glideth

Along by the groves where his Ing'borg bideth,

Thinks how last summer each evening fair,

With her beside him he wandered there.

"Where is she? Guesses she not her lover

Is near her, safely the blue waves over?

Perhaps, removed from her Balder's care,

She strikes the harp in the palace, where

Her grief she'd lessen, her needle plying."

Then sudden rises his falcon, flying

From temple turret, then downward flits

To Fridthjof's shoulder, and there he sits,

As was his wont, of his love to assure him.

From Fridthjof's shoulder can none allure him,

He scratches fast with his gold-tipped claws,
He gives no quiet, he makes no pause.
To Fridthjof's ear now his beak he bendeth,
Perchance some loved one a message sendeth;
Is it Ingeborg? Wildly his pulses bound,
But none interprets the broken sound.

Ellide gayly the headland rounding,
Skips lightly on, like a roebuck bounding.
Familiar waters surround the prow
Where happy Fridthjof is standing now.
He rubs his eyes and his hand he places
Above his brow to discern the traces
Of home so dear; but he looks in vain,—
Of Framness ashes alone remain.
The naked chimney stands lone and dreary,
Like warriors' bones of their grave-mounds weary;
The garden place is a blackened floor,
The ashes whirl round the wasted shore.
In bitter mood from his ship he hasteth,
Around the ruins his eyes he casteth,
His father's dwelling, his childhood's pride.
Then faithful Bran, with the shaggy hide,

Comes running toward him, each moment faster,—
Of forest bears had he oft been master;
How high he springs in his gladsome glee,
How leaps with pleasure his friend to see.
The milk-white steed he so oft had ridden
Comes bounding up from the valley hidden,
With swan-like neck and the frame of a hind
And gold mane floating upon the wind.
He curves his neck and he stamps while standing,
His food from Fridthjof's own hand demanding;
But Fridthjof, poorer by far than they,
Has nought to give them,—he turns away.

Unsheltered, sorrowful stands the rover;
He looks at the meadow and grove burnt over,—
Of Hilding's coming quite unaware,
His foster-father with silver hair.
"At what I see I can scarcely wonder,
When eagles flit then their nests are plunder.
'Tis Helge's deed lest the land be wroth,
So well he keeps his crowning oath!
To hate mankind and to gods be loyal,
While blackened homes mark his progress royal!

More grief it gives me and less of pain;
But where does my Ingeborg meanwhile remain?"
"The word I bear," Hilding said in sadness,
"I fear will bring you but little gladness.
You scarce had sailed when king Ring came on,
Five shields I counted against our one.
In Disar-dale did we prove our valor,—
The river foamed with a crimson color.
King Halfdan's jest and his laugh arose,
So too the sound of his manly blows.
My shield I held as a buckler o'er him,
Well pleased with fruits his bravery bore him.
Not long indeed did the battle last,
King Helge yielded, and flying fast,
Though asa-blood in his veins was welling,
In passing Framness he fired the dwelling.
Before the brothers the choice was placed,
To give their sister to Ring, disgraced,
(By her alone could his wrongs be righted),
Or give their throne for his offer slighted.
Then hither and thither the messengers hied,
But now has Ring carried home his bride."

"O woman, woman!" said Fridthjof, scorning,

"Old Loke's thought should have been a warning;

His thought a lie, was in woman's form,

To man he sent it his heart to warm,

A blue-eyed lie that with tears alarms us,

Forever cheats and forever charms us;

A rose-cheeked lie with bust defined,

Of spring-ice virtue and faith like wind;

From out whose heart folly often glances,

On whose fresh lips basest falsehood dances.

And yet how dear to my heart was she!

And dear as ever she still must be.

My wife I've called her since in the wildwood,

We played together in happy childhood.

Of high achievement if e'er I thought,

Her love alone was the prize I sought;

As stems which grow from one root together,

If Thor strikes one then they both will wither;

If one its vesture of emerald shows,

The other mantles with green its boughs.

Our lives in joy and in grief thus blended,

I cannot think of the union ended.

But I'm alone.   O, thou noble Var

Who wanderest over the earth afar,

To record on gold every vow that's spoken,

Forego thy pastime, the vows are broken.

The tablet filled with but falsest lies,

The faithful gold 'gainst the insult cries.

Of Balder's Nanna I've oft been dreaming,

But truth in mortals is only seeming.

In faithfulness can no heart rejoice

Since falsehood borrows my Ingeborg's voice,—

A voice like wind which o'er flower fields strayeth

Or harp-strings' music when Brage playeth.

I'll list no more when the harp is tried,

I will not think of my faithless bride;

Where storms are raging there will I follow,

Till blood thou drinkest, thou ocean billow.

Where swords sow seeds for pale death to reap,

On mount or vale I my vigil keep.

If king I meet and to combat dare him

I smile to think how my sword shall spare him.

But if in battle a youth I meet,

With heart enamored and visions sweet,

Deluded fool who on faith relieth,

I'll hew him down e'er the vision flyeth,

11

Will kindly slay him ere yet he be
Deceived, disgraced and betrayed like me."

"The blood that's youthful no boundaries heedeth,"
Old Hilding said, "how much it needeth
The cooling touch of the snows of age.
You wrong the maid with your senseless rage.
My foster-daughter beware of blaming
For adverse fortune which, heaven ordaining,
The wrathful norns upon men below
Hurl down, for none can escape the blow.
Like silent Vidar, no outward token
The maiden gave that her heart was broken.
Her grief was mute as in southern grove
The voiceless woe of the widowed dove.
To me alone who her childhood guided
Was all the pain she endured confided.
As dives the sea-fowl with wounded breast
Lest daylight's eye should upon it rest,
And there remaineth with life-blood flowing,
No sign of weakness or misery showing,
So she in darkness her suffering bore,
And only I saw her anguish sore.

She often said: 'I am but an offering

For Bele's kingdom; who talks of suffering!

The snow-drop fragrant, with leaf and vine

To deck the victim in wreaths they twine.

How sweet to die and escape from anguish!

But no, in pain must I live and languish;

For Balder's wrath will no rest allow

My aching heart and my throbbing brow.

But tell to no one my secret sorrow,

I'd rather suffer than pity borrow;

King Bele's daughter her fate may dare,—

But kindly greeting to Fridthjof bear.'

The wedding day with its footsteps fateful

Arrived at last. O, the day most hateful!

To the temple marched in procession sad,

The white-robed virgins and men steel-clad;

A bard dejected the train was guiding,

The pale bride followed, a black steed riding,—

As pale was she as the wraith which sits

On a storm-cloud black, when the lightning flits.

From off the saddle I gently took her,

Nor at the temple door forsook her;

But led her up to the altar, where

Her vows she uttered in accents clear.

And long she prayed, on good Balder calling;

All cheeks save hers felt the tear-drops falling.

When Helge saw on her arm your band,

He tore it off with an angry hand;

On Balder's image now hangs the jewel.

My wrath burst forth at this act so cruel;

My sword was by me, I drew it forth,—

King Helge then was but little worth.

'Let be,' said Ing'borg, in accents broken,

'My brother might surely have spared this token;

How much one suffers ere death sets free,—

The Allfather judgeth .'twixt him and me.'"

"The Allfather judgeth," said Fridthjof slowly,

"I too would give him my judgment lowly.

Is't not now mid-summer, Balder's feast?

And in the temple the crowned priest,—

The king, who sold the maiden tender?

Ah! yes, my judgment I fain would render."

XIII.

BALDER'S FUNERAL PILE.

MIDNIGHT'S sun on the mountain lay,
  Blood-red was its gleaming;
It was not night nor was it day,
  But just between them seeming.

Balder's bale-fire, symbol bright,
  On sacred hearth was burning,—
Soon is quenched its wasted light,
  Hoder's reign returning.

Priests around the temple wall
  Burning brands were grasping;
Silver-bearded, old men all,—
  Their hard hands flint knives clasping.

The crowned king stands the altar near;
  Hark! the midnight soundeth,—
With clash of weapons, sharp and clear,
  The sacred grove resoundeth.

" Bjorn, stand fast by yonder door,
   No one must pass under,
Whosoe'er would cross the floor,
   Cleave his skull asunder."

Helge paled; he knew too well
   Whose that voice so ringing.
Forth stood Fridthjof; his fierce words fell
   Like autumn storm winds singing.

" Here's the ordered tribute; it came
   Safe through the tempest's rattle;
Take it; then here by Balder's flame,
   For life or death we'll battle.

" Shields behind us, our bosoms free,
   Fair the fight be reckoned;
As king, the first blow belongs to thee,
   Mind thou, mine's the second.

"Caught at last is the wily fox,
   Vain all thought of flying;
Think of her with the golden locks,
   Of Framness wasted lying."

Thus he spake, and the purse he'd brought,
    Forth he quickly drew it,
Careless of the mischief wrought,
    In Helge's face he threw it.

Darkness swam before the eyes
    Of asas' kinsman sainted;
Blood gushed forth, he could not rise,
    But near his altar fainted.

"With the gold you as tribute claim,
    Are you overpowered?
None shall Angervadil blame
    For felling such a coward.

"Silence, priests with altar-knives,
    Moonshine princes, quiet!
Else my sword may drink your lives;
    Thirsting 'tis to try it.

"Holy Balder, thy wrath forbear,
    Nor 'gainst me enrol it;
But the arm-ring which you wear,
    Yonder craven stole it.

"Not for thee did Volund old
    Work its fair dimensions;
The maiden wept, but the thief was bold;
    Away, such false pretensions."

Bravely drew he; together fast
    Arm and ring seemed growing;
Angered Balder, when loosed at last,
    Fell 'mid the embers glowing.

Hark! each flame, as it leaps on high,
    A golden tooth resembles;
Bjorn, all pale, stands the doorway nigh,
    Fridthjof, anxious, trembles.

"Open, Bjorn, let the people go,
    By watchmen unimpeded;
The temple burns; throw water, throw
    The ocean full, if needed."

Now a chain is knit to the strand,
    Not a link is missing;
Flies the billow from hand to hand
    Against the fire-brands hissing.

Fridthjof sits like the god of rain
    High o'er beam and water,
Gives to all his orders plain,
    Calm amid the slaughter.

Vain! the fire has the upper hand,
    Smoke-clouds dense are growing,
Gold falls fast on the red-hot sand,
    Silver streams are flowing.

All is lost! to the half-burned hall
    A fire-red cock is clinging,
He sits and crows on the roof-peak tall,
    His loosened pinions swinging.

The wind-blown flame mounts the vaulted sky,
    Everything it levels,
Balder's grove is summer dry,
    The hungry fire-king revels.

Fiercely leaping from height to height
    Aiming yet still higher;
O, what wild and terrific light!
    Strong is Balder's pyre!

Hark, it crackles! the roots now burn,
  The tops are fiery showers;
Muspel's ruddy children spurn
  Man's mere human powers.

A fire-sea billows in Balder's grove,
  Strandless breaks and hisses,
The sun is up, but bay and cove
  Mirror flaming abysses.

Soon in smoldering ashes lay
  Grove and temple's adorning;
Sadly then Fridthjof turned away,—
  Wept in the light of morning.

XIV.

FRIDTHJOF GOES INTO EXILE.

ON deck at night
In summer bright
Sat Fridthjof grieving;
Like billows heaving,
Now wrath, now grief,
In his heart was chief;
And shoreward turning
Saw fires still burning.

"Thou temple reek
Fly up and seek
High Valhal's towers;
The White God's powers
Call down on me
With wrath's decree.
And tell, swift bounding,
The vault resounding,

The temple burned
To dust is turned;
The imaged glory
But lives in story.

Quick burned the god
Like common wood.
The grove protected
Nor once neglected
Since men swords bore
Is now no more;
By fire the slaying
Not time's decaying.

Forget no word
Thou hast seen or heard,
In Balder's dwelling
The story telling,
Thou message cloud
Of gods the shroud.

Long live in story
King Helge's glory,
Who exiled me
From him and thee,
My father's nation.

We'll roam creation
Where blue is king,
Where wild waves sing.
Thou canst not rest thee
Ellide, haste thee;
Earth's farthest bound
We'll sail around.
Soon thou'lt be rocking,
The sea-foam mocking,
My dragon good;
A drop of blood
Will nothing hinder
As on we wander.
In fiercest storm
Art thou my home;—
The one I cherished
By Helge perished.
Thou art my North
My foster-earth,—
The other leaving
I wander grieving;
My bride caressed
In black robes dressed;

The one in lustre
I could not trust her.

Thou ocean free,
Unknown to thee
Is king oppressive,
Untrue, aggressive.
Thy king is he
Among the free
Who trembles never
How high soever,
With wrath oppressed,
Heaves thy white breast.
Blue fields are charming
And not alarming;
There heroes plow
With keel and bow,
And blood-rain showers
In oaken bowers.
The good steel blade
Is seed-corn made.
The fields bring yearly
Not honor merely,

But gold as well.

Oh, kindly swell,

Thou ocean billow!

Thee will I follow.

My father's grave

Calm waters lave,

(How still he sleepeth

Where green grass creepeth)

Mine blue shall be,

Flecked like the sea;

Forever floating,

On tempest gloating,

And fathoms deep

Draw men to sleep;

To me thou'rt given

For life a haven;

My grave thou'lt be,

Thou ocean free!"

Thus inly burning

Sang Fridthjof, turning

His prow so true

From seas he knew,

And slowly creeping
'Mid rocks still keeping
Their faithful ward
O'er shallow fjord.
But vengeance watcheth;
King Helge fetcheth
Ten dragons out.
The people shout,
With breath abated:
" The king is fated;
He offers fight,
We scorn his might;
Though heaven-descended,
His reign is ended;
From earth we know
He now must go.
The blood god-given
Now longs for heaven."

Scarce was it spoke
Ere keels of oak
By unseen power
Began to lower;

Then on and on

Are downward drawn

To Ran's safe keeping.

King Helge, leaping,

Is glad to swim

From the sinking stem.

And Bjorn, none blaming,

Laughed loud, exclaiming:

"Thou asa-blood,

The art was good;

No one detected,

Or e'en suspected,

I bored so quick,—

A worthy trick!

May waves enfold them

And Ran still hold them

As heretofore.

It grieves me sore

That Helge misses

False Ran's cold kisses."

In wrathful mood

King Helge stood

From death delivered;

His round bow quivered,

Though made of steel,

As toward the shoal

So hard he drew it,

Though scarce he knew it,

It clanging broke.

Then Fridthjof spoke,

His lance well aiming,

While loud exclaiming:

"A death-bird here,

Enchained I bear;

If once set flying,

Then low is lying

Thy coward head.

By Loke led

Thy fear abuseth;

My lance refuseth

A coward's blood;

It is too good

For food so craven;

Its worth be graven

On funeral stone,

But not upon

A name which beareth

The stain thine weareth.

One exploit brave

Sank 'neath the wave;

The next one failed thee,

Nor aught availed thee;

Thy bow rust broke,

Not thou. The stroke,

When I aspire,

Is set much higher,

As thou mayst see

'Tis far from thee."

His carved oar limber

Was fir-tree timber,—

A mast-fir tall,

From Gudbrand's dale.

Taking another,

With both together

He rowed amain;

Like arrowy cane

Or steel blade brilliant
Were the oars resilient.

The sun climbs up
The mountain slope,
The winds, advancing
From land, to dancing
In morning's light
The waves invite.
Where foam-crest swimmeth
Ellide skimmeth
On joyous wings;
But Fridthjof sings:

"Thou front of creation,
　Exalted North!
I have no station
　On thy green earth.
Thy lineage sharing
　My pride doth swell,
Thou home of daring!
　Farewell, farewell!

Farewell thou royal
  Valhalla-throne!
Thou night's-eye loyal,
  Midsummer sun!
Thou sky unclouded
  As hero's soul!
Thou vault star-crowded!
  Farewell, farewell!

Ye mountain ranges
  Where honor dwells,
Creation's changes
  Your rune-face tells.
Ye lakes and highlands
  I knew so well,
Ye rocks and islands,
  Farewell, farewell!

Farewell ye grave-mounds
  Where the linden showers
Near azure wave-bounds
  The dust of flowers!

But time revealeth
And judgeth well
What earth concealeth;
Farewell, farewell!

Farewell ye bowers,
    Beneath whose shade
So many hours
    By brooks I've played;
Ye friends of childhood,
    Ye meant me well,
I love your wildwood;
    Farewell, farewell!

My love is cheated,
    My home is burned,
My shame completed,
    I'm exiled, spurned.
From land appealing
    To ocean's swell,
Life's joyous feeling,
    Farewell, farewell!

XV.

THE VIKING CODE.

NOW he floated around on the desolate sea, like a
prey-seeking falcon he rode,
To the champions on board he gave justice and law;
wilt thou hear now the sea-viking's code?

"Make no tent on thy ship, never sleep in a house, for
a foe within doors you may view;
On his shield sleeps the viking; his sword in his hand,
and his tent is the heavenly blue.

"See how short is the shaft of the hammer of Thor, but
an ell's length the sword blade of Frey;
'Tis enough, for your weapon will ne'er be too short if
you dare near the enemy stay.

"When the storm rageth fierce, hoist the sail to the top,—
O how merry the storm-king appears;
Let her drive! let her drive! better founder than strike,
for who strikes is a slave to his fears.

"Never take on thy vessel the land-sheltered maid; were
    she Freyja herself she'd ensnare;
For the dimples she wears are but pitfalls for men, and
    a net is her free flowing hair.

"Wine is Allfather's drink, and the cup is allowed if you
    only can use it with sense;
He who falls on the land may arise,—who falls here he
    to Ran, the sleep-giving, goes hence.

"If a merchant sail by, you must shelter his ship, but
    the weak will not tribute withhold;
You are king of the waves, he a slave to his gains; and
    your steel is as good as his gold.

"Let your goods be divided by lot or by dice, how it
    falls you may never complain;
But the sea-king himself takes no part in the lots,—he
    considers the honor his gain.

"If a viking-ship come, there is grappling and strife,
    and the fight 'neath the shields will rejoice;
If you yield but a pace you are parted from us; 'tis the
    law, you may act by your choice.

"If you win, be content; he who praying for peace
　　yields his sword, is no longer a foe;
"Prayer's a Valhalla-child, hear the suppliant voice; he's
　　a coward who answereth no.

"Wounds are viking's reward, and the pride of the man
　　on whose breast or whose forehead they stand;
Let them bleed on unbound till the close of the day, if
　　you wish to be one of our band."

Thus his law was enrolled,— and his name, every day,
　　through all foreign coasts grew renowned;
For his like was not seen on the blue-rolling sea, nor the
　　valor his champions crowned.

Then he sat by the rudder and sullenly gazed in the
　　depths of the blue rocking tide;
·"Thou art deep; in thy depths thriveth peace, it may
　　be, but it thriveth not here where we ride.

"Is the White God enraged? Let him take up his sword,
　　I will fall if it thus is designed;
But he sits in the skies, and the thoughts he sends
　　down which forever are clouding my mind."
13

When the conflict came on, then his spirit arose like an
 eagle refreshed for its flight;
And his brow it was clear, and his voice it rang high,—
 like the thunderer first in the fight.

So from conquest to conquest unbroken he went, and
 was safe o'er the high, foaming grave;
And he saw in the south many islands and rocks, till
 he came to the calm Grecian wave.

When he saw the green groves that stand out from the
 waves, and the temple before him uprose,
What he thought Freyja knows, and the poet knows too,
 and the lover, he knows, ah! he knows!

"Here we ought to have dwelt, here's the island and
 grove, here the fane as my father set forth.
It was here, it was here I invited my love, but the cruel
 one staid in the North.

"Surely peace has its home in those blissful green dales,—
 in the colonnades, memory's words;
Like the whisper of love are the murmuring founts, and
 a bride-song the voice of the birds.

"Where is Ingeborg now? Hath forgotten me quite for
    the gray-haired and withered old king?
I can never forget, but my life I would give, if one sight
    of my love it would bring.

"Now three years have passed by since the land I beheld
    where heroic achievement prevails;
Tower the honored mounts yet to the heavenly blue? is
    it green in my forefathers' dales?

"On the grave where my father is laid I once planted
    a tree; can it be it lives now?
And who cares for the weakling? Thou earth give it
    moisture, and dew, kindly heaven, give thou.

"But why linger I longer on far distant waves, taking
    tribute and striking men down?
For my soul but despises the glittering gold, and I've
    gained quite enough of renown.

"There's a flag on the mast and it points to the North,
    in the North is the land I hold dear;
I will follow the course of the heavenly winds, and back
    to the Northland I'll steer."

XVI.

FRIDTHJOF AND BJORN.

FRIDTHJOF.

B JORN, I am weary of riding the sea,
  Turbulent fellows, these billowy fountains;
  Northland's firm earth and her long cherished moun-
    tains,
Wondrous attractions, are calling to me.
  Happy is he by his land unrejected,
No one denies him his father's green grave;
  Too long, alas, have I wandered dejected,
Outlawed, afloat on this wilderness wave.

BJORN.

Good is the sea, your complaining you squander,
  Freedom and joy on the sea flourish best;
  He never knoweth effeminate rest,
Who on the billows delighteth to wander.
  When I am old, to the green growing land
I too will cling, with the grass for my pillow;

Now I will drink and will fight with free hand,
Now I'll enjoy my own sorrow-free billow.

FRIDTHJOF.

Now hath the ice indeed chased us to land,
    Close round our keel are the stiffened waves dozing;
    Let me not waste the long winter reposing
Here among rocks on this desolate strand.
    Let me once more keep the Yule banquet olden,
Guest of king Ring and the bride of my choice;
    Let me once more see those waving locks golden,
Hear the sweet tones of that well-beloved voice.

BJORN.

Good! to king Ring it shall be my glad duty,
    Something to teach of a wronged viking's power;
    Fire we the palace at midnight's still hour,
Scorch the old graybeard and bear off the beauty.
    Or, being viking you may think it right
Honor to grant the old man by a duel;
    Challenge him out on the ice for a fight,—
Whatever you will, only waiting is cruel.

FRIDTHJOF.

Speak not of firebrands, to war give no thought,—

   Peace would I bear to the king, and not terror;

   Ring nor his partner committed the error—

Heavenly vengeance my punishment sought.

   Little of hope is now left worth the telling,

Only farewell would I take of my dear,—

   Final farewell! When the green buds are swelling,

Sooner it may be, you'll see Fridthjof here.

BJORN.

Fridthjof, 'tis time for your folly's abating;

   Sigh and lament for a false woman's loss!

   Earth is, alas, but too full of such dross;

One may be lost, still a thousand are waiting.

   Say but the word, of such goods I will bring

Quickly a cargo,—the Southland can spare them,

   Red as the rose, mild as lambs in the spring;

Then we'll cast lots, or as brothers we'll share them.

FRIDTHJOF.

Bjorn, you're as frank and as joyous as Frey,

   Bold to wage war and with wisdom advising;

Odin and Thor you ne'er think of despising,—
Freyja, the heavenly, you dare to gainsay.

Let us not question her power supernal,
Rather beware lest we waken her ire;

Once, though now slumbering, the sparkle eternal
Mortals and gods shall enkindle to fire.

BJORN.

Go not alone, lest return be prevented.

FRIDTHJOF.

Singly I go not, my sword goes with me.

BJORN.

Hagbert, remember, was hanged to a tree.

FRIDTHJOF.

Who can be taken, to hang has consented.

BJORN.

Fallest thou, then, on thy murderer fell
Carve I the blood-eagle, vengeance bestowing.

FRIDTHJOF.

Needless, fond Bjorn, he'll not hear the cock crowing
Longer than I do. Farewell, fare thee well.

XVII.

FRIDTHJOF COMES TO KING RING.

KING Ring in state was seated at Yule-time drinking
mead,
And with him sat his consort, so white and rosy red;
They seemed like Spring and Autumn, when both together seen,—
The king was chilly Autumn, fresh Spring the fair young
queen.

A man, unknown, there entered within the spacious hall,
From head to foot enveloped, a bear-skin covering all;
And though by staff supported, and bent with age and
care,
He stood a head the taller than any champion there.

He chose for seat to rest him a bench beside the door,—
'Tis now the poor man's station, as 'twas in days of yore;
The courtiers all laughed loudly, with many a gibe and
jest,
And with the finger pointed to him in bear-skin dressed.

The stranger's eyes flashed lightning which made his
 anger felt,
And quick a young man seizing with one hand, by the belt,
Both up and down he turned him; then ceased the glee-
 ful din,
For all the rest were silent,— so you and I had been.

"What causes such an uproar? who dares disturb our
 peace?
Old man, come here and answer, and let the tumult cease;
Your name, your place, your errand; come, answer if
 you can."
Thus spake the angered monarch to the half-concealed
 old man.

"You ask me many questions, I'll answer every one:
My name (I will not give it) belongs to me alone;
My birthplace was misfortune, my heritage is want,—
I hither came but lately from wolf so fierce and gaunt.

"In youth I rode a dragon upon the waters blue,
Its wings were stout, and gayly and safely too it flew;
But crippled now and frozen, it leaves the land no more,
And I, grown old and weary, burn salt upon the shore.

"I came to see thy wisdom, renowned so far and wide;

And when they met me rudely (for scorn I'll not abide),

One idiot by the girdle I grasped, and turned him round,

For that I beg your pardon,—though now he's safe and

    sound."

"Thy words are wisely chosen," said Ring, "I must agree;

The aged should be honored, come sit thee here by me;

Slip off these false disguises and let thy form appear,—

Disguise is foe to pleasure, and pleasure ruleth here."

The guest now loosed the bearskin,—it fell from off his

    head,

Where stood old age decrepit, each saw a youth instead,—

From off whose noble forehead, and round whose shoulders

    brave,

The light locks fell and floated in many a golden wave.

In azure velvet mantle, he then stood forth erect,

His belt a silver girdle with forest beasts bedecked,—

Embossed by cunning workman, each figure deftly traced,

And round and round the hero they each the other

    chased.

A massive golden circlet his sinewy arm displayed;

His battle-sword hung by him as though the lightning
stayed;

A hero glance about him he cast from time to time,

And stood as Balder beauteous, as Asa-Thor sublime.

Surprised, the queen's cheeks quickly with changing color
glow,

As northern lights so ruddy paint fields of driven snow;

As two twin water lilies, alarmed by tempest's swell,

Stand swinging on the billow, her bosom rose and fell.

The horn a shrill blast sounded, then silence reigned
throughout;

The hour for vows was coming, and Frey's boar now
they brought;

His mouth contained an apple, wreaths on his neck were
laid,

His four knees bent beneath him upon a silver cade.

King Ring, his gray locks flowing, arose and straightway now

The boar's head gently touching, he thus declared his
vow:

"I swear to conquer Fridthjof, the champion in war,
So help me Frey and Odin, and likewise mighty Thor."

Then with a smile defiant uprose the stranger tall,
A look of wrath heroic spread o'er his features all,—
He smote with sword the table till through the hall it
    rang;
And up from oaken benches the steel-clad warriors sprang.

"And now, sir king, please listen while I my vow shall
    tell,—
Young Fridthjof is my kinsman, and so I know him well;
'Gainst all the world I'll shield him, I give you here my
    word,
So help me now my norn, and likewise my good sword."

The king then laughed. "Right daring, methinks, your
    speech," said he,
"But in this Northland palace shall all fair words be free;
My queen, fill him a bumper of wine, the very best,—
I hope that through the winter he'll here remain our guest."

The queen then took the goblet, before her it was placed,—
A rare and costly jewel, which once the ure's head graced;

It stood on feet of silver, and on its golden bands
Were runes of high achievement, engraved by skillful hands.

With downcast eyes she reached him the goblet, brimming
    filled,—
But with a hand so trembling that wine thereon was
    spilled;
As evening's shades so ruddy upon the lilies glow,
So gleamed the drops of ruby on hand as white as snow.

The guest the horn accepted with reverential bow,—
Not two men could have drained it, as men are reckoned
    now,—
Without an instant's waiting the strong man, at a draught,
The lovely queen to honor, the brimming ruby quaffed.

The skald at table seated, his waiting harp brought forth,
And sang a heartfelt story of true love in the North,—
Of Hagbert and of Signe; and at the deep tones' peal
Each warrior's heart was melted, though clad his breast
    in steel.

He sang of Valhal's mansions, of heroes' blest reward,
Of ancient deeds of valor, on fields of wave and sward;

Then grasped each hand its sword-hilt, then flashed each
    eye intent,—
And quickly round the table the foaming mead-horn
    went.

And lively was the drinking within that royal hall,—
An honest Yule carousal engaged the champions all;
The sleep that followed after no care or anger stained;
But Ring, the aged monarch, with Ingeborg remained.

XVIII.

THE RIDE ON THE ICE.

KING RING to a banquet his queen would take,
The ice like a mirror o'erspread the lake.

"Go not on the ice," said the stranger bold,
"It may break, and the bath is too deep and cold."

"The king," answered Ring, "is not easily drowned,
Whoever is fearful let him go round."

The stranger was angered and sullen frowned,—
Then quickly his skates to his feet he bound.

The sledge-horse sets out, he is strong and free,—
His nostrils are flaming, so glad is he.

"Strike out," cried the monarch, "my charger good,
And show if you are of the Sleipner blood."

As swift as a storm on the sea his speed;
The prayers of the queen does the king not heed.

The stranger in mail on his skates is not still,
But passes them swiftly whenever he will.

He writes many runes on the ice besides,—
And over her name lovely Ingeborg rides.

They swiftly speed onward, the lake to span,
But under them lurketh the treacherous Ran.

Her silvery roof in a trice she breaks,
And catches the sled in the hole she makes.

The cheeks of the beautiful queen turn pale;
Then comes like a whirlwind the skater in mail.

He buries his skate in the ice, to clasp
The steed's flowing mane in his iron grasp.

With one single effort his arm he swings,
And charger and sled to the firm ice brings.

"That stroke," said Ring, "was a noble one,—
Not Fridthjof, the strong, could have better done."

So they all returned to the house of the king,—
The stranger remaining until the spring.

XIX.

FRIDTHJOF'S TEMPTATION.

SPRING is coming, song-birds twitter, woods are leafing,
 smiles the sun;
Dancing downward, toward the ocean, see the loosened
 rivers run;
Glowing like the cheeks of Freyja, from the buds the
 roses ope,—
Hearts of men to life awaken, full of courage, love and
 hope.

Ho! the chase! the aged monarch with his queen will
 go to-day;
Now in crowds the court assembles, waiting in confused
 array,—
Bows are clanging, quivers rattling, steeds impatient paw
 the ground;
Hooded falcons, wildly shrieking, make the echoing hills
 resound.

See! the queen appears! Poor Fridthjof, do not thither
  cast your eye;
Sits she on her milk-white palfrey like a star in spring's
  clear sky,—
Half a Freyja, half a Rota,— lovelier far than either one,—
From her dainty hat of purple, plumes are waving in the
  sun.

Look not on those eyes so heavenly,—of those golden
  locks beware!
Oh! take care! that form is supple, full that bosom, oh!
  take care!
Look not where the rose and lily shifting hues alternate
  fling;
Listen not to those loved accents, sighing like the winds
  of spring.

Now the hunting troop is ready. Hark, through hills
  and valleys all
Sounds the horn, the falcon loosened straight ascends to
  Odin's hall;
Forest denizens in terror haste to seek their cavern-homes;
But, with spear outstretched before her, each valkyrie
  swiftly comes.

Aged Ring no longer follows where the eager hunter flies;

By his side alone rides Fridthjof, silent, grave, with downcast eyes.

Darkest thoughts, and full of anguish, stir within his sorrowing breast,

And wherever he may wander, haunting voices banish rest.

"Oh, the sea! why did I leave it? thus to my own peril blind!

Sorrow thrives not on the billow, scattered 'tis by every wind.

Broods the viking?—danger cometh bidding him the lance prepare;

Vanish then all sad reflections, blinded by the weapon's glare.

"Here, a longing, past describing, flaps its wings about my brow,

And like one asleep and dreaming, to and fro I wander now;

Balder's precincts I remember, nor forget the oath she gave,—

'Twas the gods, not she who broke it,—gods relentless as the grave.

"For they hate the race of mortals, on their joy with
    anger look,
So to deck cold winter's bosom, they my tender rose-bud
    took;
What does Winter with my blossom? Can he under-
    stand its worth?
Nay, but bud and stem and leaflet, clothes in ice with
    frosty breath."

Thus bewailed he. Soon they came into a dark and
    lonesome dell,
Gloomy, crowded 'twixt two mountains; o'er it densest
    shadows fell.
Then the monarch halted, saying: "See how lovely, fresh
    and deep!
I am weary and would rest me, fain would have a mo-
    ment's sleep."

"Sleep not here, for hard and chilly is the ground, O
    king, indeed;
Up, thy sleep will not refresh thee, let me back the
    monarch lead."
"Like the other gods, sleep cometh unexpected. Does
    my guest,"

Said the king with feeble accents, "grudge his host a moment's rest?"

Fridthjof then took off his mantle, and outspread it 'neath a tree,
And the king, in trusting friendship, laid his head on Fridthjof's knee;
Soon he slept as sleeps the hero after battle's rude alarms
On his shield, or as an infant cradled in his mother's arms.

As he slumbers, hark! there singeth from a branch a coal-black bird;
"Hasten, Fridthjof, slay the gray-beard, free your mind by discord stirred;
Take the queen, she's thine by promise; thee the bridal kiss she gave,
Human eyes do not behold thee; deep and silent is the grave."

Fridthjof listens; hark! there singeth from a branch a snow-white bird:
"Though no human eye behold thee, Odin sees and hears each word;

Coward, wilt thou murder slumber? Slay an old de-
fenceless man?

Win what else, the crown of heroes is not won by such
a plan."

So sang both the birds, but Fridthjof, snatching up his
battle-blade,

Flung it from him with a shudder, far into the gloomy
glade.

Black-bird flew away to Nastrand, airily the other one,

Singing, sweetly as a harp-tone, straightway mounted
toward the sun.

Suddenly the old man wakens. "Much that sleep was
worth to me;

Guarded by a brave man's weapon, sleep is sweet beneath
a tree.

Yet I do not see your weapon; where has fled the lightning's twin?

What has parted you who never in your lives have
parted been?"

"Little matters it," said Fridthjof, "'tis not hard to find
a sword;

Sharp its tongue, O king, and never speaks for peace a
    single word;

Haunted 'tis by evil spirit, black, from Niflheim it
    roams,

Sleep is here in danger from it, seeking silver locks it
    comes."

"I, O youth, have not been sleeping, but to prove you
    have I tried;

(Man or sword a wise man testeth, ere in them he can)
    confide.

You are Fridthjof; since you entered first my hall I've
    known you well;

Ring, though old, at once detected what his guest would
    fain conceal.

"Wherefore, thus into my dwelling, crept you nameless,
    in disguise?

Wherefore but to cheat and rob me, and my bride bear
    off a prize?

Honor, Fridthjof, sits not nameless, hospitality's rude
    guest;

Bright its shield as sun at noonday, on its face all eyes
    may rest.

"Fame had told us of a Fridthjof, whom both men and
  gods revere;
Shields he cleft and temples wasted, bold and brave,
  without a fear.
Soon with war-shield, so I reasoned, he will come against
  my land;
And he came, but clad in tatters, beggar's staff within
  his hand.

"Wherefore now cast down your eyelids? Once, like you,
  I too was young;
From the first is life a struggle, and fresh youth its
  Berserk-gang.
Hardly pressed and tried it must be, that its onset
  triumph not;
I have proved you and forgiven, I have pitied and forgot.

"Now am I grown old and weary, in the grave shall rest
  me soon,
Therefore take, O youth, my kingdom, take my queen,
  she is thine own;
Be my son, till then remaining still my guest as heretofore,
Swordless champion shall protect me and our feud exist
  no more."

"As a thief," said Fridthjof sadly, "came I not, O king,
    to thee;

Had I wished thy queen to capture, tell me, who had
    hindered me?

But my bride, though lost forever, wished I to behold
    once more;

Fool was I! anew I kindled flames which were half
    quenched before.

"In thy halls too long I've tarried; here I must no longer
    stay.

Gods unreconciled their anger rest upon me day by day;

Balder, with the light locks flowing, loveth all mankind
    but one;

Only I am now rejected; see, he hateth me alone!

"Yes, I set on fire his temple. Fane-profaner call they me.

Children shriek when I am mentioned, joy and gladness
    from me flee;

Northland casteth out the lost one, and in anger cries—
    depart!

In my native land I'm outlawed, I am outlawed in my
    heart.

15

"I will seek for peace no longer on the earth, so green
and sweet,
Trees no more their shade afford me, burns the ground
beneath my feet.
Ingeborg I've lost forever; she, my bride, accepted Ring,
From my life the sun has vanished, night and noonday
darkness bring.

"Therefore hence to ocean's billow! Out, away my dragon
good,
Bathe again thy pitch-black bosom in the briny boiling
flood;
Wave in clouds thine inky pinions, let the sea a path
prepare,
Fly as far as star can guide us, far as conquered billows
bear.

"Let me hear the rolling thunder, let me hear the lightning's voice;
When it thunders all around me, Fridthjof's heart will
then rejoice;
Clang of shields and rain of arrows! Let the sea the
battle fill;
Purified, I'll then fall gladly, reconciled to heaven's will."

XX.

KING RING'S DEATH.

GOLDEN mane flowing,
Skinfaxe duteous
Draweth the spring sun more bright than before;
Morning beams glowing
Doubly as beauteous,
Sport in the hall;—there's a knock at the door.

Though his heart grieveth,
Enters the stranger;
Pale sits the king, while the queen's gentle breast
Billow-like heaveth;
Singeth the ranger
A song of departure, with sorrow oppressed.

"Bathes now the billow
Winged steed flying,
Sea-horse is longing to flee from the strand;
Glad will he follow

Him who is hieing
Far from his home and his well beloved land.

" The arm-ring I give thee,
Ing'borg, receive it.
Holiest memories with it remain.
Ne'er let it leave thee;
Fridthjof, believe it
Truly forgives.   Thou'lt not see him again.

" No more beholding
The smoke's upward motion
Northland I'll see.   Truly man is a slave ;
Fate is unyielding ;
Far on the ocean
There is my fatherland, there is my grave.

" When in your roaming
Stars the vault cover,
Go not with Ingeborg down to the strand ;
Lest in the gloaming
You should discover
Fridthjof, the outlawed, cast up on the sand."

"Sad is the hearing,"

Ring said, replying,

"When a man moans like a weak maiden's sigh.

Valhal is nearing,

E'en now the sighing

Death song I hear. Every mortal must die.

"No one can frighten,

Or by complaining

Change the allotment the norns have set down;

Sorrow thou'lt lighten

O'er the land reigning,—

Take thou my queen, for my son guard the crown.

"True is it spoken,

Loved and respected

Peaceful I've reigned, over mountain and vale;

Yet have I broken

Shields, unprotected,

Landward and seaward, without turning pale.

"Now shall the bleeding

Geirs-odd relieve me,—

Dying in bed ill befits Northland's kings;

　　Not worth my heeding,

　　Death shall receive me,—

Life's pain is equal to that which death brings."

　　Then carved he rightly

　　Letters all glowing,—

Death runes to Odin on arm and on chest;

　　Shine now so brightly

　　Blood-drops o'erflowing,

Dyeing the silvery hair on his breast.

　　"Bring for my drinking

　　The horn with wine flowing;

Skoal to thy honor, thou land of my birth!

　　Minds deeply thinking,

　　Harvest fields growing,—

Peaceful exploits have I loved on the earth.

　　"Vain amid slaughter

　　Bloody and daring,

Sought I for peace,—she fled in dismay.

　　Now the mild daughter

Of heaven appearing,
Beckons me hence to Valhal away.

"Hail ye immortals!
Sons of high heaven!
Earth disappears; Gjallarhorn to a feast
Opens the portals;
By the gods given,
Blessedness crowns as a helmet the guest!"

Speaking intently,
Ing'borg's hand loyal,
Also his son's, and his friend's, too, he pressed;
Eyelids close gently,—
Spirit so royal
Flies with a sigh to the Allfather's breast.

XXI.

RING'S DRAPA.

SEPULTURED sits he,
Sovereign descended,
Battle sword by him,
Buckler on arm ;
Chafes his good charger
Champing impatient,
Pawing with gold-hoof
The gate of the grave.

Ring, great in riches,
Rideth o'er Bifrost ;
Bends with its burden,
Bridge of the gods.
Wide for his welcome
Valhal it opens,
Hands to the hero
Heaven extends.

Absent is Asa-Thor,

Active in warfare.

Beckoned by Odin

The beaker is brought;

Frey the king graces

With garlands of grain-ears,

Blossoms the bluest

Binds Frigg therein.

Graspeth the gold-string,

Gray-bearded Brage,

Stiller now sigheth

The song than before;

Freyja the faithful,

Fondly reclining,

Bends o'er the board and

Burneth to hear.

"Sing high the smiting

Of sword upon helmet,

Boisterous billows,

Bloody for aye;

Power, the gift of

Gods ever gracious,

Bitter as berserk
Biting the shield.

" Hence was the hero-king,
Heaven-born dear to us,
Showing his shield
A shelter for peace.
Power's embodiment
Plainly impersonate,
Soared like a sacrifice-
Smoke to the sky.

" Words full of wisdom
Wise Odin chooseth
Sitting with Saga
Sokvabek's maid.
Such, too, the saying
Spoke by the monarch,
Fair as of Mimer
Flows the clear fount.

" Forsete faithful
All feuds adjusteth,
Sitting serenely

By the side of Urd's spring;
Thus high enthroned
Thou, king beloved,
Potently pleaded
For peace in the land.

"Niggard in nothing,
Near and far strewed he
Beauty and blessing,
Bought with his gold;
Gave he most gladly
Guerdon unstinted,
Sadness he solaced,
Suffering relieved.

"Welcome, thou wisest
Winner of Valhal!
Long thou'lt be lauded,
Loved of the North.
Brage, the bearded,
Bears thee the mead-horn,
Favored of fortune,
Friend from below."

XXII.

THE KING'S ELECTION.

"TO thing! to thing!" from dale to hill
        The cry arose.
"King Ring is dead; his place to fill
        A king we'll choose."

From off the wall the peasant moves
        His steel sword blue;
Its edge his practiced finger proves,
        It biteth true.

The boys admire in pleased surprise
        The gleaming blue;
To lift the sword one vainly tries,
        It needeth two.

The daughter scours the helmet clean,
        Bright shall it be,
And blushes, in its silvery sheen·
        Her face to see.

At last he takes his shield so round,
 A sun in blood;
"Hail! iron man, so strong and sound,
 Thou peasant good!

Renown and power which nations wield
 From thee they draw,
In war thou art thy country's shield,
 In peace its law."

The assembly met, while sounding high
 Were arms and shields,
In open thing, 'neath heaven's sky,
 In fair green fields.

Upon the thing-stone Fridthjof stands,
 And with him there
A little one with shining bands
 Of golden hair.

Then rose the cry on every hand:
 "Too small indeed
The king's son is to rule our land,
 Our wars to lead."

But Fridthjof on his shield raised up
    The little boy:
"Ye Norsemen, here behold your hope,
    Your king, your joy.

"High Odin's race embodied here
    In image see,
As much at home 'mid shield and spear,
    As fish in sea.

"I swear my lance and sword to set
    Round land and throne,
And with the father's coronet
    To crown the son.

"The oath I make to Balder's son*
    Of high renown,
And if I fail, may he not shun
    To strike me down."

The boy sat on the shield so high
    As 'twere a throne,
Undaunted as the eaglet's eye
    Looks toward the sun.

* Forsete.

At last impatient grew his blood,
    And to the ground,
The child leaped down and fearless stood;—
    A kingly bound!

Then rose the cry from all the thing:
    "We of the North,
We choose but thee, be like king Ring,
    Thou shield-borne youth.

"And Fridthjof shall a guardian be,
    Thy youth to guide;
His mother, earl, we give to thee,
    To be thy bride."

But Fridthjof frowned: "To-day," said he,
    "Election make,
But not a bridal; leave to me
    A bride to take.

"To Balder's temple I'll repair,
    I go to see
The norns who are already there
    Awaiting me.

"With them a council I have willed,
    The shield-maids true,—
Beneath the tree of time they build,
    Above it too.

" Against me Balder's anger sore
    Doth still abide;
He took, he only can restore
    My cherished bride."

Saluting then the monarch new,
    He kissed his brow,
And o'er the broom-heath passed from view,
    Silent and slow.

XXIII.

FRIDTHJOF AT HIS FATHER'S GRAVE.

"HOW brightly smiles the sun, so friendly seeming,
  As swift from branch to branch its soft rays glide!
Allfather's light within the dew-drop gleaming,
  Is clear and pure as in the ocean wide.
See! all the mountain tops with red are streaming,—
  From Balder's altar flows the bloody tide;
In night will shortly sink the world's commotion,
As sinks the golden shield beneath the ocean.

" Yet let me first behold those well known places,
  My childhood friends that I have loved so well;
The same sweet beauty still the valley graces,
  The same birds yet alight in wood and dell;
The same blue wave the stable rock embraces,—
  Oh, would I ne'er had tried its treacherous swell!
It always speaks of fame and high endeavor,
But far from home it bears thee on forever.

16

"I know thee, stream, whose waters erst were freighted
  With swimmer bold, who with thy billows fought!
I know thee, too, thou vale where oft we plighted
  Eternal faith! Alas! earth holds it not!
Ye birchen trees, whose bark I carved delighted
  With many runes, still wedded to the spot
Your white stems stand, crown-capped with sunshine
    golden,
All save myself unchanged since days now olden.

"Is all unchanged? Where, then, is Framness' dwelling,
  And Balder's temple on the sacred shore?
At thought of childhood's dales my heart is swelling,
  But fire and sword devoured them, they're no more.
Of human vengeance, of God's wrath their telling
  To wanderers over blackened field and floor;
Thou pious pilgrim, come not here to ponder,
For forest beasts in Balder's grove now wander.

"With Nidhug's curse each human life is teeming,—
  The cruel tempter from the land of shade,
He hates the asa-light with glory beaming
  On hero's brow and on his shining blade;

Each coward deed, each act of wrathful seeming,

Is his, a tribute unto darkness paid;

He wins when temples burn and gods are slighted,

He claps his coal-black hands and laughs delighted.

"Is there no expiation, radiant heaven?

Thou blue-eyed god, dost thou no penance take?

Man pardons man who has for pardon striven,

When men atone the gods their wrath forsake;

By thee, the mildest one, I'm unforgiven;—

Command, and any sacrifice I'll make;

No will had Fridthjof in the temple's burning;

Oh! stainless make his shield, thine anger turning.

"Thy burden take away, I cannot bear it,

The dark wood's music in my soul doth cry.

A moment's fault! cannot a life repair it,—

An upright life? Then hear my contrite sigh!

If Thor's fierce bolt should strike, I still would dare it;

Nor shrink to meet the look of Hel's pale eye.

Thou pious god, who moonlight glances bendest,

'Tis thee I fear, and vengeance which thou sendest.

"My father's grave is here. The hero sleepeth;—
    Alas! whence he has gone none ever roam;
A starry tent his home, no more he weepeth,
    Where shields rejoice and brimming mead-horns foam;
Thou asa-guest, from heaven look down where keepeth
    His weary watch thy child. O father, come!
I bring not runes nor charms, but bending lowly
Would learn to appease pale Balder holy.

"Still silent is the grave? Ah yes, and cruel.
    A sword roused Angantyr within his grave;
A sword is naught,—Tirfing a trifling jewel
    Compared with what I ask. A sword the brave
Can gain on battle field or in a duel,—
    Forgiveness from the asas' home I crave;
Bear thou my plea, my sorrowing look to heaven,
No rest have noble minds if unforgiven.

"Thou'rt silent, father! Hear the waves resounding,
    And send thy loving word by their sweet cry;
Now flies the storm, on its swift pinions bounding,
    O, whisper to me as it flieth by;

See golden rings the western sky surrounding,

    Let them the message give which words deny.

No sign or answer for thy son forsaken ?

How poor indeed are those whom death has taken !"

The sun is quenched. The evening breeze is stealing

    Upon earth's children with its lullaby,

And sunset tints in myriad circles wheeling

    Around the brim of heaven's rosy sky,

O'er hill and dale their azure hues revealing,

    A vision now of Valhal passeth by;

Then unexpected comes with rustling motion,

An image, gold and flames from western ocean.

A wondrous Hagring now the heavens covers,

    (The name that Valhal gives hath lovelier sound),

And over Balder's grove it gently hovers,—

    A golden chaplet set in emerald ground;

Resplendence everywhere the eye discovers,

    Such lustre mortals ne'er before had found.

It stops and sinks to earth, not disappearing,—

But where the temple stood, a temple rearing.

An imaged Breidablik its wall upreareth,

    (So burnished silver on the cliff had shone),

Each pillar cut of deep blue steel appeareth,

    The altar is a single precious stone,

A power unseen the vaulted roof upbeareth,—

    A winter sky with sparkling stars o'erstrewn;

And there with golden crowns and robes befitting,

Of azure splendor, Valhal's gods are sitting.

With rune-writ shields, the maids of fateful power,

    The noble norns, within the portal stand,—

Three rosebuds springing in a single flower,

    A grave and yet a fascinating band;

While Urd is pointing to the ruined tower,—

    The new one Skuld doth greet with welcome hand;

But scarce restored is Fridthjof, filled with blended

Delight and wonder, ere the scene is ended.

"From you, Time's maidens, comes illumination,—

    Thine, hero-father, is the token good;

The wasted shrine I'll build on sure foundation,

    In beauty shall it stand where erst it stood;

How excellent to thus make expiation,

    By peaceful deeds to atone for actions rude!

The outcast still may hope who sues in meekness,—

The White God softens, and forgives his weakness.

"All hail, ye myriad stars in splendor beaming!

    With joy I watch you silent tread the skies;

And welcome, Northern-lights, above me streaming,—

    No more a flaming temple to mine eyes;

Grow green, O grave! and from the wave bright gleaming,

    Thou wondrous melody again arise.

I'll sleep upon my shield, and dream how heaven

Forgets the faults its mercy hath forgiven."

XXIV.

TIIE RECONCILIATION.

COMPLETED now was Balder's temple. Not enclosed
As heretofore with fence of wood; of hammered steel,
With golden knobs upon each bar, was built the fence
Round Balder's ground.   Like steel-clad champions
    ranged for war,
With halberds and with golden helms, there stood it now
On guard around the sanctuary of the god.
Of giant stones alone the massive wall was built,
And joined with active skill,—a noble giant work
For all eternity (as is Upsala's shrine,)
Where Norseland saw its Valhal in an earthly mold.
It stood there in its grandeur on the mountain cliff,
And mirrored in the ocean wave its lofty brow,
While round about it, like a zone of beauteous flowers,
Far stretched the dale of Balder with its sighing groves,
Its song of birds, a home where peace might reign supreme.
High rose the copper-bolted portal, and within
Two colonnades supported on strong omoplates

The vaulted canopy, and beautiful it hung

Above the temple, like a concave shield of gold.

At farthest end stood Balder's altar. It was hewn

From one huge block of northern granite; round it coiled

A graven serpent, covered o'er with written runes,—

Profoundest thoughts from Vala and from Hávamál;

But in the wall above was left an open space,—

A dark blue ground all filled with golden stars; and there

A silver image sat—the pious god—as calm

And mild as sits the silver moon in heaven's blue.

Thus seemed the finished shrine. In couples entered now

Twelve temple virgins, clad in robes of silver gauze,

With roses glowing on their cheeks, and roses in

Their guileless hearts. Before the image of the god,

Around the altar newly consecrate they danced,

As light spring winds above the flowing fountains flit,

As dance the forest elves amid the waving grass,

While yet the morning dew, like pearls, lies glittering there.

And while they danced they joyful sang a sacred song

Of pious Balder, and how dearly he was loved

By every being; how he fell 'neath Hoder's dart,

And earth and sea and heaven wept. Yet sounded not

The song as though 'twere uttered by a human voice,

17

But as a tone from Breidablik, from Balder's home;
Or like the thought of lover to a lonely maid
When pipes the quail his deep notes in the hush of night,
And over northern birches falls the moonlight soft.
Enraptured Fridthjof stood; he leaned upon his sword,
And gazed upon the dance. Sweet childhood's memories
    thronged
His vision by,—an innocent and pleasant folk,
With smiling eyes reflecting heaven's blue, with heads
Surrounded by a halo of bright locks, they waved
A kindly salutation to their childhood's friend.
Then sank the bloody shadow of his viking life,
With all its conflicts, all its perilous exploits,
Down into night, and in his fancy stood he forth
A flower-crowned monument above their grave.
And ever, as the song increased, his spirit soared
From earthly dales below to Valaskjalf above;
Then melted human hate and human vengeance, too,
As melts the icy coat of mail from off the cliff,
When shines the sun in spring. A sea of quiet peace,
Of silent ecstasy, possessed his hero-soul;
It was as if he felt the heart of nature beat
Against his own; as if, deep moved, he fain would fold

Creation in his brotherly embrace, and be at peace
With every living creature seen of God.
Then came into the temple Balder's priest most high,
Not young and beauteous as the god, but tall in form,
With heavenly mildness beaming in his noble face,
While down about his girdle flowed his silver beard.
An unused reverence possessed proud Fridthjof's heart;
The eagle wings upon his helmet meekly drooped
Before the aged man, who thus spoke words of peace:
"Son Fridthjof, welcome hither — I've expected thee;
The strong man gladly roves around the earth and sea,
A berserk-like, who pallid bites the shield's hard edge,
But weary grown, and thoughtful, wanders home at last.
The powerful Thor went many times to Jotunheim,—
But spite his belt divine and gloves of finest steel,
Still sits the Utgard-Loke on his lofty throne;
For evil is itself a power, and will not yield,—
And piety not joined with power is children's play;
'Tis like the sunbeams on the breast of Æger thrown,—
An image faint, which falls and rises with the wave,
Foundationless and insecure, devoid of trust.
But power not joined with virtue eats itself away,
As rust the buried sword. 'Tis life's unchecked carouse;

The heron of oblivion hovers o'er the cup,

And when the drinker wakes, he blushes for his deed.

All power is from the earth of Ymer's body formed;

Wild waves and flowing waters are the veins therein,

From various metals are its tough strong sinews forged,

And yet 'tis empty, desolate, unfruitful, till

The sun its light and warmth, heaven's piety, sends down.

Then spring the grass and flowers a web of many hues;

The tree lifts up its crown and knits its golden fruit,—

And man and beast are nourished at the mother's breast.

'Tis thus with every child of Ask. Opposing weights

Has Odin laid within the scales of human life,—

And when they balance true, then even stands the beam;

And heavenly piety and earthly power they're called.

The power of Thor is great whene'er about his loins,

Immovable, he girds the belt of strength and strikes.

Indeed is Odin wise, when Urd's clear silver fount

He looketh down, and birds swift flying come to bring

The asas' father tidings from the world's extreme;

Yet both turned pale, the radiance of their starry crowns

Was half extinguished when the pious Balder fell,—

The band was he of all the diadems of heaven.

Then withered on the tree of time its splendid crown,

And Nidhug gnawed upon its root; then were loosed
The powers of aged night. The Midgard serpent flung
Toward heaven its poison-swollen tail, and Fenris howled,
And Surt's swift fire-sword flashing gleamed from Muspel-
    heim.
Since then wherever thou mayest look the strife goes on,
A war throughout creation. In Valhal crows
The cock with golden comb. Upon and 'neath the earth
The blood-red cock to battle calls. There once was peace
Not only where gods dwell, but also on the earth;
In man's as in the high gods' thoughts was peace.
Whate'er has happened here below has also chanced
In greater measure there; humanity is but
An image frail of heaven; it is as Valhal's light
Reflected in the shield of Saga writ with runes.
Its Balder hath each heart. Remember'st thou the time
When dwelt within thy breast sweet peace a guest, and life
As joyful seemed, as heavenly calm, as song bird's dream
When summer night-winds to and fro so gently wave
Each fragrant blossom sleeping in its bed of green?
Then holy Balder still abode in thy pure soul,
Thou asa-son, thou wandering image of high heaven.
For childhood Balder is not dead, and Hela gives

Again her prey as often as a child is born.

With Balder also groweth up in every soul

His brother Hoder, blind, the child of night; for blind

At birth is evil always, like the young of bears, and night

Its mantle, but the good of earth rejoice in light.

The tempter, busy Loke, always ready stands

To guide the blind one's murderous hand.   The missile oft

To Valhal's love is sent, to Balder's tender breast.

Then Hate awakes and Violence upon its prey

Springs forth; the hungry sword-wolf prowls o'er hill and
     dale,

And fiercest dragons wild swim o'er the bloody waves.

For this meek Piety a powerless shadow sits

One dead among the dead, and with him pallid Hel,

And in its ashes Balder's sanctuary lies.

So too the asa's life on high prefigures that

Mere human life below, and both are but the thoughts,

The silent thoughts of Odin which can never change.

What hath been, what shall be, that the song profound

Of Vala knows,—Time's lullaby, its drapa too.

Creation's annals have a melody the same,

And man may hear his own life's history therein.

Dost comprehend or not?   'Tis Vala asketh thee.

Thou seek'st atonement; know'st thou what atonement is?

Oh, Fridthjof, look me in the eye and turn not pale!

Round earth a mediator goes, his name is Death.

A spark translucent, from eternity, is time;

/ All earthly life is but the refuse from Allfather's throne;

Atonement is to there return all purified.

The lofty asas fall themselves, and Ragnarok

The day of their atonement is, a bloody day

On Vigrid's hundred miles of plain; there will they fall,

But fall not unavenged, for there the evil die

Forever, but the fallen good arise again,

Refined, from out the flaming pyre to higher life.

'Tis true the star-crown, pale and withered, falleth down

From heaven's temple; earth too, sinks beneath the sea,

But brighter is it born again, and joyous lifts

Its flower crowned head from out the seething waves,—

And new created stars pursue with god-like glance

Their silent pathway round about the new-born earth.

/ But on the green hill-slopes will Balder govern then

The new-born asas, and a human race renewed.

The golden tablets filled with runes, lost long ago,

In Time's fresh morning, then are found amid the grass

On Ida's plain, by Valhal's children reconciled.

The fallen good in death are only tried by fire;

It is atonement made, a birth to higher life,

Which, purified, flies back to him from whom it came,

And plays a guileless child upon its father's knee.

Alas! that all the best is found beyond the grave,—

That gate of green which Gimle opens; vile is all,

Contaminated all that dwells beneath the stars.

And yet there is atonement found in life itself,—

A humble prelude to the peace of heaven above.

'Tis like the broken chords the minstrel strikes upon

The harp, when he with skillful fingers wakes the song;

The tone attuning with a gentle hand, before

With firmer touch he grasps the golden strings,—

Grand memories of old alluring from their grave,

While Valhal's splendor streameth on enraptured eyes.

For earth, indeed, is only heaven's shadow, life

The grounds in front of Balder's temple in the sky.

The people sacrifice unto the gods; the steed

Bedecked with gold and purple is an offering made.

A token this with meaning most profound,—for blood

Tints red the morning light of each atonement day. .

But signs are not the substance, they can not atone,—

Thine own transgressions no one can amend for thee.

In Odin's breast divine the dead are reconciled;

Atonement for the living lies in their own hearts.

One offering, I know, unto the gods more dear

Than smoke of victims. 'Tis the sacrifice of thine

Own vengeance, and thy heart's untamed and bitter hate.

Canst thou not silence them, and canst thou not forgive,

O youth? What wilt thou then in Balder's sacred house?

With what intent hast thou this holy temple reared?

With stones is Balder not appeased. Atonement dwells

Below, as up above, alone where dwelleth peace.

With all thy foes and with thyself be reconciled,

The light-haired god will then be reconciled with thee.

They have a Balder in the south,— the virgin's son,

Who by the Allfather wise was sent to explain the runes

Upon the norns' black shield rand,— unexplained before.

His battle-cry was peace, his conquering sword was love;

And blameless sat the dove upon his silver helm.

He holy lived and taught, he died and he forgave,—

And under distant palms his grave in sunlight lies.

From dale to dale his followers wander, it is said,

And melting hardened hearts, and laying hand in hand,

Establish peace upon the reconciled earth.

I do not know the doctrine well, but dimly have I

In my better moments guessed what it may mean,—

And every human heart at times divines as well.

I know the time will come when it will lightly wave

Its white dove-piniqns over all our northern hills;   .

But that day come, the North will be no more to us;

The oaks will sigh above our long-forgotten graves.

Oh, fortunate and blessed race! Ye who shall drink

The sparkling beaker of that light, I bid you hail!

It will be well if it can drive away the cloud

Whose humid covering hitherto has veiled life's sun.

But scorn not us, who, in sincerity, have sought

With unaverted gaze to find the light divine.

The Allfather is but one, though many herald him.

"Thou hatest Bele's sons. And wherefore hatest thou?

Because to thee, a yeoman's son, they did not choose

To give their sister, who belongs to Seming's race,—

The noble son of all-wise Odin. Their descent extends

To Valhal's throne,—and pride of birth is theirs.

Thou sayest that birth on fortune, not on worth, depends.

Of merit all his own, O youth, is no one proud,—

But only of his fortune; for the best of things

Are only God's good gifts to man. Art thou not proud

Of thy heroic deeds, of thy superior strength?

Who gave thee thy great strength? Did Asa-Thor not
 knit

Thy sinewy arms as firm and close as oaken boughs?

And is it not God's spirit high which joyous beats

Within the citadel of thine arched breast? Is not

The lightning God's which flashes in thy fiery eyes?

Beside thine infant cradle sang the haughty norns

The prince-song of thy life; for that thy merit is

No whit the greater than the king's son's for his birth.

Lest thy pride be condemned another's censure not.

King Helge now is fallen."

     Here broke Fridthjof in:
"King Helge fallen? When and where?"

       "Thou canst but know

That while thou here wert building, he was on the march

Among the Finnish mountains. On a lonely crag

There stood an ancient shrine,—to Jumala 'twas built

Abandoned long ago,—the door was now fast closed;

But just above the portal still there stood a strange

Old image of the god, now tottering to its fall.

But no one dare approach, for there a saying rife
Among the people went from age to age, that he
Who first the temple sought should Jumala behold.
This Helge heard, and, blinded by his furious wrath,
Went up the ruined steps against the hated god,—
Intent to cast the temple down. When there arrived
The gate was closed,— the key fast rusted in the lock.
Then grasping both the door-posts, hard and fierce he
     shook
The rotten pillars. All at once, with horrid crash,
Down fell the ponderous image, crushing in its fall
The Valhal-son. And thus he Jumala beheld.
A messenger last night arrived the tidings bore.
Now Halfdan sits alone on Bele's throne. To him
Thy hand extend, to heaven thy vengeance sacrifice.
That offering Balder asks, and I, his priest, require
In token that the peaceful god thou mockest not.
If thou refuse, this temple then is built in vain,
And vainly have I spoken."

                 Then stepped Halfdan in,
Across the copper threshold, and with doubtful look
He stood aloof from him he feared and silence kept.

Then Fridthjof loosed the breastplate-hater from his side,

Against the altar placed his shield's bright golden orb,

And weaponless approached his silent waiting foe.

"In such a strife," said Fridthjof, in a kindly voice,

"The noblest he who offers first his hand for peace."

King Halfdan blushed, then off he drew his glove of steel,

And hands long separated met in friendly clasp,—

A hearty hand-shake, steadfast as the mountain's base.

And then the aged priest revoked the ban which on

The outlawed temple-violater long had lain.

'Twas scarce dissolved ere entered Ingeborg, attired

In bridal robes and ermine mantle, with her maids,—

So glides the moon, whom stars attend, in heaven's vault;

With tear-drops in her lovely eyes, she fell upon

Her brother's neck; but he, with deep emotion, laid

His sister, grown more dear, on Fridthjof's faithful breast;

And o'er the altar of the god she gave her hand

To him, her childhood's early friend, her heart's beloved.

GLOSSARY.

For such explanations as are not found in the original notes we are chiefly indebted to Prof. R. B. Anderson, of the University of Wisconsin, and to his valuable work, NORSE MYTHOLOGY. We are also under obligations to Mrs. E. Hasselqvist, of the Augustana College of Rock Island, Illinois.

ÆGER. The god of the stormy sea.

ÆGER'S BOSOM. The sea.

ALFHEIM *(elf-home)*. Frey's dwelling.

ANGANTYR. A champion who was slain in a duel by Hjalmar the vigilant, and was buried with his sword Tirfing. His daughter Hervar called upon her dead father for the sword, and, according to the story, was answered. *See Canto XXIII.*

ANGERVADIL *(grief-wader)*. Fridthjof's sword.

ASA. God. It is used as a prefix, as Asa-Thor, Asa-Loke, etc.

ASA-SONS. A people who came from Asia and settled the North, and who claimed descent from the gods.

ASGARD. Home of the gods.

ASK. The first man.

ASTRILD. Cupid.

BALDER *(the best)*. The mildest, the wisest and the most eloquent of the gods. He is the god of innocence, the White God.

" Balder dies in nature when the woods are stripped of their foliage, when the flowers fade and the storms of winter howl. Balder dies in the spiritual world when the good are led away from the paths of virtue, when the soul becomes dark and gloomy, forgetting its heavenly origin. Balder returns in nature when the gentle winds of spring stir the air, when the nightingale's high note is heard in the heavens, and the flowers are unlocked to paint the laughing soil, when light takes the place of gloom and darkness. Balder returns in the spiritual world when the lost soul finds itself again, throws off the mantle of darkness, and like a shining spirit soars on wings of light to heaven, to God who gave it."—*See* NORSE MYTHOLOGY, p. 294.

BAUTA-STONE. A rough stone set up at warriors' graves, and having no inscription.

BERSERK *(bear-coat)*. The old Northern athletes or champions wore the skins of bears, wolves or reindeer, and went into battle with loud cries, wearing no armor.

BERSERK-GANG. The onset of the berserks.

BIFROST *(the trembling way)*. The rainbow, the bridge of the gods.

BJORN *(a bear)*. Notice the play upon this word in Canto X, p. 95:

"*Bjorn* attend the rudder,
Grip it with a *bear's* paw."

BLOOD-EAGLE. When a foe deserved especial cruelty, he was put to death by carving the picture of an eagle on his back.—*See Canto XVI*, p. 151.

BRAGE. God of poesy; a son of Odin.

BRAN. Fridthjof's dog.

BREIDABLIK *(broad-gleaming)*. Balder's abode.

BURN SALT. A common expression for making salt.

DELLING *(day-spring)*. Dawn.

DELLING'S SON. Day.

DISARSAL. The temple of the goddesses.

DRAGON. A war vessel.—*See description of Ellide, Canto III*, p. 30.

DRAPA. A funeral hymn, reciting the virtues of the deceased.

EFJE-SOUND. A sound in the Orkney Islands.

FAFNER. A son of Hreidmar and brother of Regin and Otter. Fafner and Regin demanded of their father a share of the gold obtained of Odin as Otter's ransom. Hreidmar refused, and Fafner slew his father, and, taking all the gold, assumed the form of a dragon and fled. He concealed the gold on Gnita heath, where he was found by Sigurd, who, at the instigation of Regin, slew Fafner. He accomplished this by digging a pit in Fafner's path and concealing himself therein until the dragon passed over him, when he thrust his sword through Fafner's heart. *See* NORSE MYTHOLOGY, p. 377; also the story of the Volsungs and Niblungs, translated by Magnússon and Morris. Sweden, 1870.

FAFNER'S BANE. The slayer of Fafner; Sigurd.

FENRIS. A wolf, and one of Loke's children. Chained by the gods until Ragnarok, he gets loose and conquers Odin, but is himself slain by Vidar.

FOLKVANG *(the folk-field)*. Freyja's dwelling.

FORSETE *(the presider)*. Son of Balder and Nanna. The god of justice.

FOSTER-BROTHER. It was customary in the North, when two persons entered into friendship for life and death, or, as it was called, *foster-brothership*, that each wounded himself and allowed his blood to mingle with the other's. *See, concerning Fridthjof and Bjorn,* Canto III, p. 34.

FREY *(a lord)*. The god of harvests; the dispenser of wealth.

FREYJA. Frey's sister, and goddess of love.

FRIGG. The wife of Odin and mother of Balder.

FUTHORC. The runes taken collectively are properly called the *futhorc*, the word being made up of the names of the first of the runes. Compare *alphabet*.

GEFJUN. The goddess of maids.

GEIRS-ODD *(spear-death)*. Death by the spear, self-inflicted. *See Valhal.*

GERD. Frey's wife, and very beautiful.

GIMLE. The heaven of heavens, where dwell the righteous after Ragnarok.

GJALLARHORN. The horn of Heimdal, the Saint Peter of the old Mythology. It was heard all over the world.

GLITNER *(the Glittering)*. Forsete's golden dwelling.

GRONING-SOUND. A sound between the Danish Islands.

18

GUDBRAND'S DALE. Canto XIV, p. 138. In the diocese of Agger-
hus, celebrated afterward (1612) for a battle in which the
Norwegians slaughtered the forces of Col. Sinclair, the Scotch
ally of Christian IV, of Denmark.

HAGBART. A sea-king, who became secretly betrothed to Signe, a
princess, thereby gaining the enmity of her father, who cap-
tured and hung him. Signe, unwilling to survive her betrothed,
set fire to her dwelling and was burned to death.—*See Cantos
XVI and XVII.*

HAGRING. *Fata morgana.*

HÁVAMÁL. The high song of Odin, containing many wise precepts
for the government of men.

HEL. The goddess of death.

HILDER. The goddess of war.

HODER. The blind god; brother of Balder. Tempted by Loke, he
slew Balder with the mistletoe.

IDA'S PLAIN. Where the gods assemble after Ragnarok.

IDUN. Wife of Brage. She is the rejuvenating goddess, the "ever-
renovating spring, and hence she is dressed in green.—*See
Canto I,* p. 5. She keeps the apples of immortality.

JOTUNHEIM. The abode of the giants.

LOKE. The evil one. "He is the sly, treacherous father of lies.
In appearance he is beautiful and fair, but in his mind he is
evil, and in his inclinations he is inconstant. Notwithstanding
his being ranked among the gods, he is the slanderer of the
gods, the grand contriver of deceit and fraud, the reproach of
gods and men. Nobody renders him divine honors. He sur-
passes all mortals in the arts of perfidy and craft."—*See
NORSE MYTHOLOGY,* p. 373.

MIDGARD. The earth; the abode of man.

MIDGARD-SERPENT. A child of Loke. It was cast into the sea by
Odin, and it grew till it reached around the whole world.

MIMER. The wise giant keeper of the holy well of wisdom.

MORVEN'S HILLS. Hills in the north of Scotland.

MUSPELHEIM. The abode of fire.

MUSPEL'S SONS. Flames.

NANNA. Balder's wife; goddess of flowers. She died heartbroken at Balder's death.

NASTRAND *(the shore of corpses).* Where the wicked are punished after Ragnarok.

NIDHUG. The dragon which lives in the fountain Hvergelmar and gnaws the root of Ygdrasil.

NIFLHEIM. The world of mists; the lower world; the place of punishment.

NORNS. The Fates. They are three: Urd, the past; Verdande, the present, and Skuld, the future. They control the destinies of gods and men.

ODER. Freyja's husband.

ODIN. The chief of the gods. He is the all-pervading spirit of the world, the governor of the universe, the author of war and the inventor of runes and of poetry. In appearance he is old, tall, one-eyed and long-bearded. He wears a broad-brimmed hat and a many-colored coat, and carries a spear called Gungner.

ODIN'S BIRDS. Odin has two ravens, Hugin and Munin (reflection and memory), which every day fly around the world and return to him with intelligence of all that happens.

PEASANT. The piece of lowest rank in chess; a pawn.

RAGNAROK *(the twilight of the gods).* The day of the destruction of the world, and of the regeneration of gods and men. *See Canto XXIV.*

RAN *(the robber).* Goddess of the sea; wife of Æger.

ROTA. One of Valhal's maidens; a valkyrie.

RUNES. The letters of the ancient Scandinavian alphabet were called runes *(secrets).* The runes were sixteen in number, and previous to the introduction of Christianity they were supposed to have been invented by Odin himself. A knowledge of them was for a long time confined to a few, who used them for the purposes of sorcery.

RUNE-STONE. A stone inscribed with runes, and set up at graves or elsewhere as a monument.

SAGA. Goddess of history; hence a history.

SEMING. A son of Odin. The early kings of Norway traced their lineage directly to Seming.

SIGNE. *See Hagbart.*

SIGURD. The slayer of Fafner. *See Fafner.*

SKINFAXE *(shining mane).* The horse of Day.

SKOAL. A health.

SKULD. The future. *See Norns.*

SLEIPNER *(the slipper).* Odin's horse with eight feet.

SOKVABEK. Dwelling of Saga.

SURT. God of fire.

THING (pronounced ting). A deliberative assemblage of Norsemen, composed of all who were capable of bearing arms. It was held in the open air. The thingsmen expressed approval of any measure by striking the shield with the sword.

THOR. The second of the gods; the thunderer; the subduer of the frost giants. He has a red beard; his weapon is a short-handled hammer called Mjolner. He is girt with a belt of strength, and wears iron gloves. His sons are Magne and Mode, strength and courage.

URD. The past. *See Norns.*

URD'S FOUNT. The fountain from which the norns sprinkled the tree Ygdrasil.

UTGARD-LOKE. The Loke of the giants, — called *Utgard,* because he dwelt in the uttermost parts of the world, *Jotunheim.*

VALA. A prophetess.

VALASKJALF. Odin's dwelling.

VALHAL *(the hall of the slain).* Only those who fell by wounds received in battle, or self-inflicted, were entitled to the joys of Valhal, where they were feasted by Odin and attended by the valkyries.

VALKYRIES *(choosers of the slain)*. Goddesses who serve in Valhal and go on Odin's errands.

VAR. The goddess who presides over marriages.

VEGTAM. A name assumed by Odin when he went to consult the vala concerning the fate of Balder. — *See* NORSE MYTHOLOGY, p. 281.

VIDAR *(forest)*. The silent god; a son of Odin. He slays the Fenris-wolf at Ragnarok.

VINGOLF *(floor of friends)*. Freyja's dwelling.

VOLUND. A renowned smith corresponding to Vulcan.

YGDRASIL. An ash tree; the tree of the world. The norns sprinkled the top with water from Urd's fountain and thus kept it alive, although Nidhug gnawed its roots.

YMER. An enormous giant slain by the gods, and of whose body they created the world.

89009511890

www.ingramcontent.com/pod-product-compliance
Lightning Source LLC
Chambersburg PA
CBHW030114030726
47498CB00007B/2386